The Valley of the

Shadow of Death

THE VALLEY OF THE SHADOW OF DEATH:

NEPHILIM RISING

THE GUARDIANS OF LIGHT SERIES

BOOK THREE

Kasey Hill

Azoth Khem Publishing
Huntsville, AL
April 2025

AZOTH KHEM

© Azoth Khem Publishing, 2025

ISBN: 978-1-952880-26-1
First Edition 2020
Second Edition 2025

Azoth Khem Publishing
29931 Copperpenny Drive NW
Harvest, AL 35749
www.azothkhem.com

Ordering Information:
Quantity sales and exclusive discounts are available on quantity
purchases by corporations, associations, and others. For details,
contact the publisher at the address above. For orders by U.S.
trade bookstores and wholesalers, please contact
Azoth Khem Publishing: Tel: (256) 221-5498 or visit
www.azothkhem.com

Printed in the United States of America

For my Luxina

Check out these other series by Kasey Hill

The Guardians of Light Series
Firefly of Immortality
The Shining Ones
Firefly: The Half-Blood Angel
The Valley of the Shadow of Death: Nephilim Rising

Dark Woods Series
Devil's Claw

The Whispering Spirits Series
The Haunting at Foxwood Village
Dark Coven

Coming Soon to The Guardians of Light Series
Firefly of Immortality II
Black Wings of Death
Firefly of Immortality: Anniel Unveiled
Alpha and Omega
Firefly of the Apocalypse

Coming Soon to The Guardians of Light Series Universe

The Guardians of Light: Darkness Falls Series
Bloodlines: Into the Shadows

The Valley of the

Shadow of Death

PROLOGUE

IT HAD BEEN A YEAR since we escaped Alpha. Xavier and I hid in the realms of the Otherworld as we made our journey to find Starfire. Praeziel was our guide, along with Gwendolyn, as we hopped from portal to portal, trying to find the oracle's cloaked cabin. We have traveled far and wide, often crossing the same places twice, looking for her. By the time we had reached her last known place of existence, she had already fled to seek safety and refuge from Alpha. My understanding has been that Alpha knows about her and has for quite some time. It has been his plan to find her so she can help him with Damian like she is to help us.

Praeziel doesn't know much about how she is going to help us. The only thing he knows is that she is the key to unlocking our full potential. My guess is that it has to do with the faery enchantment that was placed upon our parents when they were created.

I find myself every day wondering if my parents are both okay and if Damian is being tortured anymore. We know for a fact that Alpha is still running tests and creating new species of demons. We have happened across a few of them along our travels that we had to dispatch. Damian's altered blood is now the key to these creatures, whether Alpha has perfected his serum or not. After my visions with the injections, everyone began to wonder if my mother, Sophie, had actually died or not when the Glade fell to ruin.

After we visit with Starfire, that is when the real battle of minds and wits begins.

Alongside Praeziel, we will have to convince the Nephilim to join ranks with us to help defeat Alpha. We gained alliances with Seelies and Unseelies and even mended the bonds of discrimination amongst their ranks. A new world order is coming to pass, but only if we are able to defeat Alpha in the end. If we can stave off the apocalypse that is brewing, ending the heavenly war, we will, without a doubt, be able to forge an unbreakable alliance to keep the Children of the Night and the Forsaken in the abyss with all of the other monsters Alpha created throughout time.

CHAPTER 1

"WHERE COULD SHE BE?" I asked as I loaded my arms with firewood.

Xavier and Praeziel had been slowly building us a fire for the night with what sticks we could scrounge up from the area. I dropped the firewood beside their circle of stones and dusted my hands off on my pants. A chill had filled the air, and I rubbed my arms. We were far from any trail in a remote area of the wooded hills in Europe. We had traveled through so many faery portals that I didn't even know which country we were in this time. Gwendolyn had gone to hunt us some food to roast over the fire and hadn't made it back yet. It made me nervous whenever she went off by herself. We could be ambushed at any moment of the day, and we are better in numbers. Xavier and I were the only safe ones from harm. Alpha would have Praeziel and Gwendolyn killed on-site. I couldn't live with myself knowing more people had died trying to keep us safe from Alpha.

"Gwendolyn not only goes out to hunt but to ask local fey if they have heard of anything from the trees, plants, or animals as to where she may have gone," Praeziel replied, jabbing a stick into the fire and kindling it into a roar.

"I wonder if we keep tripping her senses, and she believes we are the danger that Alpha poses," I commented, hunching down beside the warm flames.

"That could very well be," Praeziel replied, leaning back against a tree stump.

Xavier sat quietly, picking at blades of grass, lost in thought. If only I knew what went through his mind... somehow, he was able to put a block up so I couldn't hear his thoughts anymore. It happened after the escape from Stygia. I'm sure it had to do with meeting our father for the first time. Or maybe learning his mother had died. Actually, it could be a number of things, but it doesn't make the loneliness I feel any better.

"I'll take first watch tonight," Praeziel stated as he watched me yawn.

"Oh, I'm not even tired. I'm just cold," I replied with an appreciative smile, rubbing my arms again. "I don't ever recall being this cold. Where are we?" I asked.

"We are in the Netherlands," Gwendolyn replied, appearing with rabbits, squirrels, and some bird attached to strings slung over her shoulder. Her hunting bowstring rested across her chest with her quivers on the opposite shoulder, along with the prey she had hunted.

"Any word?" Praeziel asked.

"Possibly," she replied as she plopped the dead animals down in front of her. She pulled out a blade and began to skin the animals to prepare them for the fire. "I spoke with some of the river nymphs, and they heard tale that Starfire is on an island out past Australia. It's a few days' journey from here."

"That's good news, right?" I asked, looking between her and Praeziel.

They both nodded quietly and returned to the silence of the night. Xavier didn't make a sound nor acknowledge Gwendolyn's return. I could watch the air around him darken and shroud him as he thought deeper and deeper to himself.

"Xavier," I spoke aloud. He glanced up to me, bewildered, looking around. "Let's go for a walk," I said with a small smile.

"Don't stray too far," Gwendolyn ordered. "The hills around here are treacherous, and you could find yourself in a hole made by trappers."

"We'll be careful," I promised as I stood up and held my hand out to Xavier to take.

He stood along with me and walked over to me, but he didn't take my hand. His demeanor toward me had changed ever since we went to see the Dark Queen. He hardly talked to me anymore. He never held me while we slept, and any type of physical contact was put to the back of his mind. I don't know what I did to make him angry with me or to change in regards to me, but a sinking feeling always blossomed in my bosom whenever he refused my hand.

"A penny for your thoughts," I said, as we strolled silently through the trees.

He still didn't speak, and I sighed. "What's wrong, Xavier? You never talk to me anymore. What's going on in that head of yours?" I asked, peering up at him in the little bit of moonlight that breached the tops of the trees.

"I just don't have anything to say," he replied.

"Did I make you mad at me or something? It's been a year of these conversations," I asked, prodding deeper.

"You didn't do anything," he replied heatedly. "I just don't want to talk."

And with that, he stalked off back the way we came to the campsite and left me alone in the dark. Tears threatened to spill as I once again felt as if my heart was going to break in two.

"Give him time, Luxina," the voice called out in the dark.

I jerked my head around, trying to scan anywhere I could see in the dark. I knew that voice. Only one person would call me sister. Damian. But how did he find us?

"How would I not find you? You're my blood," the reply came to the silent question in my head.

I still couldn't find him in the dark, inky black of night. Was he here to steal me back away to Alpha? Was he here to kill me as he had killed Sophia?

"No and no," he replied.

I heard a twig snap, and I jerked my head in the direction it came from. There, in the low glow of the moon, I saw the red curls split through the dark trees. I was too far from the campsite to yell for help even if he did intend to hurt me. I had no weapons on me, either.

"I can sense your fear and anxiety. I assure you, sister, that I am not here to hurt you. As a matter of fact, I am here to help you put an end to Alpha's reign of terror," Damian said as he stepped into the light, and I could see his face.

I scanned it deeply, looking for a twitch or a tell-tale sign of him lying. I didn't find anything. My insides wrenched against each other as I grappled with my own fears. Could I trust him? And even though the past could clearly show I could not, something tugged at me as my heart thumped that said I could indeed trust him.

"Were you followed?" I asked, scanning the area from where he appeared in the dark.

"No. I slipped out undetected, and I am cloaked. No one, not even Alpha himself, would be able to find me by tracking my wings."

He stopped short of me with his hands clasped behind his back. I wonder if he has a weapon? As if to answer the question in my mind, he brought his hands around and showed they were indeed empty.

"I don't want to be Alpha's soldier any more than your father did," Damian stated, staring into my eyes. "I just want to be with those I care about. Not with someone who just uses me because I have special blood."

Funny enough, I believed every word he said. Even so, I had to be hesitant. I had to be sure.

"You killed Sophia. You killed Praeziel's mother," I said dryly.

"No, I did not. Sophia is safe and hidden away. I pretended to murder her to satisfy Alpha. Trust me, Luxina, she is safe and well with the Watchers that are left," he replied quietly. A few moments passed as I just stared him in the eyes. "You believe me, don't you?"

His voice was different from most of the times we talked. He sounded needy, as a child looking for approval from a parent would sound. The harsh undertones in his speech had filtered away, and a soft tone had replaced the voice of the boy that stole me away from my father. I took a deep breath and let my gut take control... or was it my heart?

"Oddly, yes. I believe you," I replied, stepping toward him. I reached my arms out to hug him, and he flinched away. I could see the terror in his eyes.

"I just want to hug you."

"Why?" he asked, looking closely at my hands, examining them for weapons.

"Because that's what people do when they care about one another," I replied as I wrapped my arms around his shoulders.

He didn't know what to do. I could tell he had never been shown affection by Alpha. He hesitated as he lifted his arms and placed them around my shoulders as well. The hug deepened, and his arms tightened around me as tears slid down his cheeks.

"I always knew you were in there, somewhere," I said as he silently sobbed into my hair.

"Alpha is so close to making the injections the right way, and I am so scared of the monster I would turn into," he cried out in breaths.

"We won't let that happen," Praeziel said, startling Damian and me from the hug.

Behind me stood Gwendolyn, Praeziel, and Xavier. I don't know how long they had been there watching. I didn't even hear them walk up. I am horrible at this whole stealth and hunting thing. Damian quickly swiped at his face, drying the tears so no one would see them.

"So, everyone is in agreement that Damian stays with us?" I asked, looking face to face.

Gwendolyn and Praeziel nodded. Xavier didn't even acknowledge the question. He just stared angrily at Damian and me. He scowled and stalked off back to the campsite alone.

"I will talk to him," Praeziel stated and sighed, heading back to the campsite as well.

"Good luck," I mumbled.

"As I said," Damian began. "Give him time."

"Easy for you to say. You haven't gotten the cold shoulder for a year now," I replied, more heated than intended. "Sorry. It just annoys me how he is acting so childish."

"He has every right to act childish," Damian replied softly and wisely. "He just lost his mother, and he doesn't know where his father is. There's more, but it's his business to bring it to light, not mine."

"The mother part, maybe. The father part, not so much. The first time he met Dad, all he did was sit and talk angrily, then glare at him. He blames everyone for growing up without a family to call his own," I said as we meandered back to the campsite.

"Don't we all," Damian whispered in reply.

I felt a pang of guilt. He and Xavier were alike. Neither grew up with their mother nor father. One grew up with Lilith, and the other grew up with Alpha. They were closer to being twins together than Xavier and I were.

"Well, I am here now. I will always be here," I replied as I took his hand in mine almost as if by instinct. "And when this is all over, you can live with us. My dad would love you as his own. You know that, right?"

He chuckled a bit. "Oddly enough, yes. I do know."

I squinted at him, wondering exactly what that meant. The last I knew of him meeting my father was the day he kidnapped me for Alpha. Based on that alone, there was no way my father would adore him, as I had stated, without getting to know the real him first. I mulled on it and let it go without prodding him further. By the time we had made it back to the campsite, Gwendolyn had the food roasting across the fire, Praeziel was watching the perimeter, and Xavier was sitting alone at a tree away from the fire. Damian dropped a bag at the tree line and took a seat near me at the fire.

"Dinner is almost ready," Gwendolyn stated, pinching the animals as they roasted. "You hungry?" she asked, looking at Damian.

A frown quickly hid the developing look of shock Gwendolyn had as she averted her eyes and looked back to the fire. I followed her gaze, looking at Damian more carefully. I nearly gasped. He was just skin and bones. Red scars littered his face as if he had been beaten with a whip. His eyes sunk in with black rings underneath them. Anger coursed through me, and steam began to rise from my skin. Damian stepped back, confused as to what he did wrong to spark such a response from me. A quick glance around the fire alluded him to the answer when no one would look directly at him. Once he realized it, he smirked a bit.

"To say I'm starving would be a bit of an understatement," he replied with a laugh.

The tension in the circle broke, and sympathy washed around everyone. I had recalled my fire back within before I burned the trees down around us. I had gotten better at controlling it with the help of Gwendolyn and Praeziel. They taught me a few calming tricks. Dad had always tried to help me, but he never could get it right. He still had troubles himself reeling in his own fire. I guess we all just had a temper with a short fuse, which is why.

Gwendolyn picked up one of the sticks that had a roasted rabbit on it and handed it over to Damian.

"Thank you," he replied as he took the stick from her.

Hungry eyes stared at the food, but his face also looked a shade of green as if the thought of food was revolting. That could be a very real possibility. I know they taught us in physical education that when the body is starved, food can make you sick.

"Take it one bite at a time," I coaxed.

He looked at me, and for the first time, the strong eyes I remembered seeing for the first time a year ago had disappeared. Before me sat a boy with puppy dog eyes, hoping that his weakness didn't make him actually weak.

"Luxina, here you go," Gwendolyn said, holding out a stick with a bird roasted on it.

"Thank you," I replied with a smile and glanced over to Xavier. "Hungry, X?" I asked.

He didn't answer me. I rolled my eyes as Gwendolyn reached over to him a stick with a squirrel on it, and he took it without offering a thank you or anything. I felt a hand brush my shoulder and knew it was Damian, reminding me again to give him time. Something tugged at my heart, and I brushed the feeling away. I stole glances at Damian as he took small bites of the food he was given. He had only eaten a small portion of the rabbit when he set it aside, propping it up against a tree, so he didn't get it dirty.

The circle was silent as everyone ate but didn't ask the lingering question in the air.

"How did I get away from Alpha?" Damian asked aloud. He smiled and chuckled a bit as we all looked a bit confused at him. "That answer is simple." He stood from his spot and stretched out his cramped legs and arms in the air before returning to his seated position. "Incaendiel helped me escape."

We all gawked at him. The question we had needed an answer to, and we finally received it. Alpha did have him. That's why he hadn't come for me.

"Is he ok?" I asked a bit too eagerly.

"He's alive." Damian wouldn't look at me. It was all the answer I needed. He may be alive, but he wasn't ok in the least bit of sense. "Alpha won't kill him. Trust me. Lucifer has tried to persuade him to let him perform the deed. He needs all of us," Damian replied. "And as for the mind-reading, no, it isn't your imaginations. I can read everyone's mind sitting around this campfire."

I glanced at Xavier to see if that bothered him. If it did, it didn't register with him. He sat silently, eating the food Gwendolyn had given him. He tossed the finished carcass off into the tree line, fixed his sleeping gear on the ground, and rolled over to go to sleep.

"I think Xavier has the right idea," Gwendolyn purred. "We should all get some rest."

"I have the first watch," Praeziel replied with a smile. "I called it already."

I had an extra bag with sleep gear in it that I had been toting in case one of ours was damaged in some way, so I tossed it over to Damian. He caught it and nodded his thanks. I put my sleeping bag on the ground where I had been sitting, unzipped it, climbed inside of it, and zipped myself back up in it. The warmth of the bag enveloped me, and I snuggled deeper down into it. Damian stretched his out right above my head and just sat on top of it. His eyes looked so sunken in with the little light the glow of the fire emitted.

"How long has it been since you slept?" I asked, propping my head in my hand.

"Who says I sleep?" he chided.

"Because you are one of us. You sleep and most likely have dreams as well," I replied softly.

He was quiet for a few minutes. I sighed in exasperation. Looks like they both will only let me in so far. I rolled onto my back and stared at what

16

few stars I could see through the canopy. I often wondered what the universe looked like from the gates of the Summit. I bet it was breathtaking. The beautiful lights of the stars dancing throughout the galaxy. The purple and pink particle clouds floating through space while comets shoot by.

"It is just that beautiful," Damian said, breaking me from my thoughts. "And I haven't slept in weeks, months before that. Not since Alpha began the torture…"

And it was back to silence. I didn't know what to say. I could only imagine what they had done to him. His own father… I drifted off to sleep with everything tumbling through my head. Damian was here. Damian was here safely. My father helped him escape. Alpha torturing him. What was he trying to get out of him? Did he know where we were, and Alpha knew? Was that what Alpha wanted from him? Maybe he stopped taking his injections.

CHAPTER 2

I KNOW I HAD to have a fitful sleep for anyone observing me while I dreamed. My dreams were terrible, horrible...

* * *

FIRE AND BRIMSTONE rained from the sky. People I had heard of were being burned to death or turned into pillars of salt where they stood. Alpha led a chariot through the sky pulled by four horses. Each horse was a distinct color. Red, white, black, and a pale gray color. The valley under him darkened as millions of werewolves, vampires, demons, and other creatures he had created ran forth, ready for battle. I stood powerless as I watched my father lead the advancing angels into the developing war of the heavens. A pit formed below their pounding feet filled with draugrs, the zombie creatures made from werewolves and vampires. I watched helplessly as they tumbled into the pit, and it filled with fire. I waited for my father to emerge from the pit. I was running to him. I was running to pull him free. But I was held back. I was trapped in tar. No matter how much my feet pulled and pulled at the thick, oily substance, I just sank deeper and deeper. I looked to my left and saw Damian and Xavier struggling just as I was in the pit. Alpha arrived with a cheerful laugh of triumph at our plight.

"Join me and be free," he yelled, laughing maniacally.

"Never!" Damian seethed. "Then die, young Shining Ones."

Alpha stared at us emotionlessly. It was almost as if something had snapped within him. He felt nothing now. It was then that we watched his plan unfold. We watched him snap his fingers, and the valley filled with lava from one side and water from another. Asteroids rained from the sky along with the fiery brimstone that had been pelting down. And I watched as the universe burned to ruins. The stars exploded in the sky. The air we breathed became toxic, and I gasped for air.

"If I can't have what rightfully belongs to me, no one will," Alpha said. "I will just start over and do it the

right way." It was then that the lava and water reached Damian, Xavier, and me in the pit.

* * *

I WOKE UP SCREAMING, gasping for air that readily filled my lungs. Tears streamed freely down my face. Hands were on me, and I fought them. It was Alpha. I knew it. He had found us. Damian had led him here. It was all part of a plan.

"Luxina!" Damian yelled as he tried to fight my arms down to my side. "Luxina, it was just a dream!! Open your eyes!"

I pried my eyes open without realizing I had been squeezing them shut from fear of what it would look like around me. I was in my sleeping bag, and Damian was above me, shaking my shoulders. I thumped my head back against the ground and let out an exasperated sigh.

"It was just a dream," I choked through tears.

Damian scooped me up in his arms and squeezed me tightly. "No," he whispered. "It was the beginning of the end."

The sun shone down on us, and the morning rays peeked through the treetops. I pulled away from him and looked deeply into his eyes. I could see the fear. I could see the agitation. I could see everything that I was feeling reflected back at me.

"That's why you don't sleep," I whispered

softly.

He nodded.

"What's going on?!" Xavier demanded as he rounded the corner and shot to the middle of the campsite.

I hadn't even realized that there wasn't anyone here except for Damian and me.

"We heard screaming," Praeziel stated as he rounded the bend right behind Xavier. "Are you ok?" he asked, eyeing Damian.

"Yeah, sorry. I, uh, had a bad dream is all," I replied. "Damian was just trying to wake me up."

Xavier glared at Damian as he stomped wordlessly back off into the woods. Praeziel just released the breath he had been holding. I knew what he was thinking. He had trusted his gut with Damian until he heard my screams. He nodded in our direction and turned to follow Xavier back into the woods.

"What were they doing?" I asked Damian.

"I have no idea. All I know is that they left at dawn, and that is the first I have seen them since," Damian replied as he went to untangle himself from my arms.

"No! Please, don't," I said as I wound my arms tighter around him. "I… you… it's just comforting." I was silent for a moment. "It's peaceful in your arms. I can't explain it. I feel calm around you. I can't imagine being without you right now, with Xavier being the way he is. You feel like home, and I don't ever want to know what that doesn't feel like… Please, just stay with me for a bit."

"Always," Damian whispered, tightening his arms around me. "I won't ever leave you."

We stayed like that for a few minutes until he pulled away, and I let him this time. I stared up at his face and wanted to cry. The fire's light showed little compared to the light of day. His entire face was sunken in. He looked like a walking skeleton. At some point in the night, he had removed his shirt to try and get comfortable, most likely. His chest, stomach, shoulders, and everything were skin and bones with large healing scars all over. I went to touch one, and he grabbed me by the wrist before I could touch him. His grip was tight and hard before he realized he was squeezing my arm too tight. My hand had begun to turn a deep red-violet when he released my hand.

"I'm sorry," he said sheepishly, rubbing his hair. "I don't like to be touched."

"No, I'm s-" He put his finger to my lips as he shushed me, looking around.

"We need to leave. Now!" he hissed, scrambling to his feet.

Xavier, Praeziel, and Gwendolyn all came bounding into the campsite.

"We have to go!" Praeziel yelled.

They all began to break down their things at the campsite as I struggled out of my sleeping bag. Damian helped me out and got it rolled up for me. He ran to his bag and rolled it up, stuffing it into the duffle bag I had given him last night. I stuffed mine into my bag as well and glanced to see that the other three had taken notice of his appearance as well and were staring at the marks on his back as they scrambled to stuff the supplies in their bags. Damian pulled his shirt on and reached into his pocket. He pulled out something that was as small and as slender as an ink pen. He pushed something on the side of it, and it transformed into the hilt of a sword, then metal materialized into a point.

"What is it?" I asked as I slung my pack on my back.

"Werewolves," Damian replied as the others slung their packs on, too.

He lifted his bag and the duffel bag I had given him from the ground and scanned the area.

"Where is the next portal?" he asked in a nervous but commanding tone.

"Just through the brush," Gwendolyn replied, pointing in the direction behind me.

He tossed me the bags, and I fumbled, catching them. "Get to it before they pick up all your scents," he demanded as he stood his ground.

I bent over, picking the duffel bag up from the

ground and balanced the load in my arms. "You're not staying behind!" I refuted. "You're coming with us!"

"I can't let them find you!" he yelled back, turning to glare at me. "You have to go now!"

"NO!" I yelled back.

"This is not a debate!" he shouted. "They can follow you into the portal. It doesn't stop them."

"Then, I will stand and fight at your side," I replied stubbornly. "We just got you. We aren't leaving you behind!"

"Luxina, get into the portal with Gwendolyn," Praeziel demanded. "Xavier and I will stay behind and help."

It was then that I heard the sounds that Damian had heard in the dead silence with his fine-tuned ears. I could hear the pounding of feet through the brush. The trees pushed back, cracked, toppled, and swayed as the herd of werewolves stampeded toward the campsite. Their snapping and snarling jaws could be heard, and their howls and growls grew louder.

Praeziel threw Xavier a sword from his side as he wielded a bow and arrow. Xavier twisted it in his hand with ease. It was then I saw they were all right. I had no battle skills. Dad had never taught me to wield a weapon. I was untrained. Damian, Xavier, and even Praeziel had all been trained in combat style. Gwendolyn most likely had been trained as well, but she was going with me to protect me from the other side of the portal. At the thought of her name, I felt her hand grab my wrist and pull me off in the opposite direction of the assailing enemies. We had breached the portal door when the first wolf tore through the brush and bounded toward Damian. I watched as he sliced the head of the beast cleanly off before three more crashed through the brush surrounding them all. Everything disappeared from view as we crossed into the portal.

Gwendolyn placed herself between the portal and me, waiting for anything to come trampling through it. The anxiety and anticipation were killing me as I waited behind her. It seemed like an eternity. The silence between us grew deeper and deeper as she waited for something to come flying toward us. When I thought I couldn't wait any longer and was about to run back out, Xavier stepped through the portal. He was covered head to toe in blood. I gasped and ran to him to inspect him for injuries.

"It's not my blood," he finally said.

I looked into his eyes to see if there was any life in them in the heat of the moment. I wrapped my arms around him, and the static between us grew. He pushed me off and walked off behind Gwendolyn. Praeziel walked through next, covered head to toe in blood and gore as well.

Gwendolyn let out a sigh of relief and ran to him, throwing her arms around her.

"Don't you ever make me leave your side again. Never again!" she said as she hugged him deeper.

He returned her hug, wrapping his arms around her. "I cannot make that promise, and you know it."

I waited for Damian to appear, but he didn't. I began to panic.

"Don't worry," Xavier said before I could ask. "He's fine. He went to search for the den. They were sent by Alpha. So, he must kill the rest of them and then hide his scent." His eyes lingered on me for a few seconds as if he wanted to say something more, but he didn't. He turned and walked to the stream off to the left of the portal to clean himself up. Praeziel went with him as well to wash up.

I released the breath I didn't even know I had been holding. Xavier and Praeziel had just finished cleaning off the blood and guts from their clothes and bodies when Damian finally stepped through the portal. He was covered in even more blood and bits than they had been. I sighed in relief as soon as I saw him. My breath caught in my throat as I looked into his eyes and saw the golden glowing light from them. He looked majestic. I had never seen that before.

"I followed their tracks for a couple of miles.

They ended in the middle of a field. It was as if they had materialized out of thin air," he said as he walked to the river to join the other two in washing up. "It doesn't make sense."

I watched as the blood pooled in the water from the three of them washing. And just as quickly as I looked, it disappeared. I looked at Gwendolyn in confusion, hoping she could or would explain.

"Nature here takes care of itself. It purged the river of the blood and sent it back to your world. The Otherworld is a special and unique place. Things that do not belong do not settle here," she explained.

I nodded in understanding. The guys were getting their clothes back on and picking their weapons up, along with the duffle bags they had.

"Let's get a move on," Praeziel stated. "We have a three-day trip to make it to Sable Island."

"Sable Island?" I asked, a bit confused. "I thought we were going to Australia."

"No, she's on an island off of Australia," Gwendolyn replied. "Most of the journey will be through the Otherworld. So, we should be safe for the time being."

I lifted my canteen from my bag and shook it. "Is the water safe for us to drink?" I asked Gwendolyn.

"This river is, yes. But always ask, so you don't accidentally drink from the poisoned ones," she replied.

I filled my canteen, and everyone else followed my example. I handed Damian the bags he had tossed at me before taking on the werewolves. He put the duffle bag over one shoulder and carried the other in his hand. Gwendolyn took the lead of our little group and led us through the forests. Xavier followed behind her with Praeziel on their heels. I hung back and walked with Damian as he took in the sights around him.

"It's beautiful here, isn't it?" I asked, looking around at the different trees and plants.

Flower petals drifted in heaps from the trees, making it look like it was snowing flowers. The aroma in the air was sweet, with a hint of death. Although they were pretty to look at, you must never touch them.

"It really is," Damian replied in awe, looking around.

A full bloom drifted down intact, and he caught it in his outstretched hand. He handed it over to me, and I felt my cheeks warm.

"Thank you," I replied, tucking it behind my ear.

"Don't mention it," he replied with a smile. His face darkened a bit. "Next time, please do as I ask. I don't want you getting hurt."

"Train me?" I asked. "I want to help, and I don't want to be useless. Dad never trained me, and I feel like a damsel in distress. You had diligent militant training."

"Why doesn't Xavier teach you?" Damian asked. "He's had ample opportunity."

"I don't know," I replied with a shrug and looked at my feet. "He hardly talks to me. What makes you think he would train me? Sometimes, I feel as if he blames me for everything that has gone wrong in his life."

"When we make it to Starfire, I will be happy to train you," Damian said.

I gave a smile that would normally be accompanied by a girlish squeal of delight but refrained from drawing attention to us. Autumn leaves now fell in heaps as the flowers had. Where the air had been warm and inviting, it now had a crisp chill to it. You could feel the impending immortal sleep for the trees to come. However, in this part of the woods, it would be forever in a perpetual autumnal state. The trees were consistently "dying off" while never fully dying. It was a rather sad notion.

The wind picked up, and dust swirled around our feet and up our bodies, bringing flower petals and fallen leaves up and over us. The sun in the sky began to grow dark as the moon of this world eclipsed it. I glanced ahead to catch Xavier's face to see if he was affected by the sights as much as Damian and I were. He seemed to walk unphased through the mesmerizing scenes of the Otherworld. He seemed more like a soldier now than the caring boy I had met in the meadow. Where light once filled his eyes, darkness now rests. It was almost as if he lived in the shadows now. Everything that had mattered was left in a city of dust that had already capsized into the wind. I just wish he could find the peace he needed. A place above the shadows that drowned him in silent sorrows. Everything he lost in the yesterdays had just damaged his tomorrows. I miss the colors of his soul that shone so brightly to me...

I returned my attention back to my walking companion, who had grown silent. I guess there's no more privacy with him around. I'm sure he was prying into my thoughts as we walked in silence.

"I was not," he laughed, breaking the quiet air.

I giggled alongside him. "Oh, now I definitely know you were." I laughed heartily, and it felt refreshing to have someone to joke with.

"I do have a question for you, though, one that that isn't related to training or anything I have been thinking about for the past, I don't know, thirty minutes?" I said as we watched the season begin to change slowly. "How long have we been walking? Time seems to stop in here."

"I think it's actually been an hour," he chuckled. "And what would that be?" he asked, quirking his lip up in a side grin.

"How did they find you?" I asked. "Aren't you cloaked like us?"

His eyes pinched together in a frown. "Yes," Damian replied. "But they can track the scent of my blood because of the injections. Blood smells blood."

"You're not one of them, Damian. You're not a monster," I replied heatedly. "It's not your fault what Alpha has done to you."

"It may not be my fault, but I am part monster until the injections can filter out of my blood. That's how I knew they were there. I could smell them," he said. "Blood smells blood."

"How can they come through the portals?" I asked. "I thought only the fey could access them. That's why Gwendolyn has led us everywhere in the Otherworld."

"They were made from Seelie blood, remember?" he replied. "So they can follow us through the portals."

"Even the original werewolves and vampires were made from Seelie blood?" I asked. "I just thought the creatures made after were made from the blood."

"That's what he wanted everyone to assume. He tried to make humans with the aid of Titania and Oberon. However, the Seelie blood mutated the humans he attempted and created vampires.

The werewolves were made from hellhounds, which are a special breed of wolf from the Otherworld. Everything always comes back to the Seelies," he explained.

"So, we aren't safe anywhere from anything that has to do with Alpha," I replied.

"No, we are not," he said, sighing. "Next time I ask you to do something, please do it without arguing. You could have been hurt back there. That is the last thing I want for you."

"I was afraid no one would stay behind to help you and would have left you to fend those beasts off by yourself," I explained.

"I could have taken them. I was thrown into the arena with werewolves as part of my training. It was like the gladiator battles except I was the only one tossed in," he replied.

Up ahead, Gwendolyn had come to nearly a full stop when Damian and I paid closer attention to our surroundings. It was dead quiet. The wind did not blow, the animals did not make noises, and even the tree branches had fallen silent. The hairs on my neck stood on end, and every nerve ending lit up with anxiety and panic.

"What is it?" I asked.

Gwendolyn held her finger up to tell me to be quiet. The panic was rising in the back of my throat. Before I could even protest her, I felt myself jerked from my feet, and I thudded to the ground with a yelp. I was dragged backward while I clawed at the ground, trying to get a grip on something to stop whatever was pulling me. A scream escaped my lips, and I rolled over to see what had a hold of me. However, there wasn't anything there. I felt a hand on my arm, and I halted in midair. I looked ahead of me. Damian had snagged my arm and had his foot firmly on a small boulder on the path.

"Hurry up!" he shouted as Gwendolyn came running to my side.

"What is it?" I screamed, kicking, trying to release my foot from whatever held it.

"I'm not sure. It's cloaked to even me. It must be from here, though. There was no way anything could have tracked us after we walked through the Forget-Me-Trees of spring. Whatever this is must be from the Nightmares and Shadow realm of the Otherworld," she replied.

"Look in my bag," Damian shouted. "There is a vial of dust. You must expose him with the dust to see him."

Gwendolyn scrambled through his bag, looking for what he said to grab. She pulled the vial from the bag and poured a handful of dust into her palm. She blew it in the direction that whatever had me would have been. The creature began to materialize. The grotesque thing in front of me couldn't even be described in words. It had tusks like a walrus, it was as tall as a troll, and it had one eye like a cyclops.

"I'm losing my grip," Damian urged as his foot slipped a bit from the rock he had wedged it against.

"I don't know how to kill this thing," Gwendolyn replied. "You're going to have to use your power."

"I can't use it without risking burning the woods down or catching you all on fire here," I retorted.

"It's your only chance!" Gwendolyn yelled as she retreated back to a safe point.

"Let me go, Damian!" I shouted.

"I'll be fine," he replied, not releasing his grip on my arm that was slowly slipping through his sweaty hands.

Before I could even summon forth the fire from my belly, a tunnel of flames flew straight toward the thing that had my leg. It dropped me immediately as the flames engulfed him. I looked back to see Xavier funneling his powers at the creature. It dropped to an ashen crisp at my feet as Damian pulled me back onto his lap. I stared at the thing, afraid to move. I looked back at Xavier as he withdrew his flames and smoldered under the sun. His eyes burned the same color Damian's had when he had walked through the portal after fighting the werewolves.

"How did you do that?" I asked in disbelief.

"Praeziel has been helping me learn to channel the flames into a usable weapon," he replied with a superior smile.

Enraged, I stood to my feet. I watched as Praeziel and Gwendolyn retreated as I felt the steam rise from skin.

"Is that what you two were doing this morning? Training?" I asked heatedly.

"Well, yes," Xavier replied. "We do it every morning."

I turned my gaze from him to Praeziel. "Is there some reason you feel it isn't necessary to include me in anything at all? You have been training him with his powers, with his fighting, but you haven't attempted once to include me in anything."

"I didn't think it would be necessary for you to train," Praeziel replied, a bit shaken.

"Why? Because I most likely won't be in the 'final battle?' Don't you think it would be necessary for me to be able to protect myself and others at all? What would have happened had Damian not been there to grab my arm at the last second? He struggled to keep me here. He struggled alone. Not one of you even bothered to run for my other outstretched hand to help pull me to safety. Gwendolyn's only offer is for me to torch the whole place and everyone standing around, hoping that you all survive. So, I ask again,

Praeziel, why do you feel it isn't important for me to even learn the basics of defense when I am at a disadvantage between the two guys that were raised with a sword in their hand?"

Silence fell over the group, and Xavier lost the grin that had painted his face a moment before. No one answered me as I stared at each of them in the circle as if they had a secret that I wasn't allowed to know.

"I'm not a fragile flower. I have powers that need to be tamed just as much as these two do. I'm tired of being an afterthought when it comes to anything that has to do with saving this universe. Do you know what my nightmare was? I was trapped and unable to help anyone else and had to watch every person I cared about die before my eyes. If you want to leave me vulnerable, fine. I will find someone who will train me the decent way."

I stood from the ground and dusted my outfit off. I picked up my duffle bag and headed toward the closest portal to the mortal world I could see.

"Where are you going?" Xavier demanded.

"Anywhere but here with you all," I replied.

"You can't enter without my help," Gwendolyn stated softly.

"Newsflash, I have Seelie blood running through my veins. I can go anywhere I damn well please," I shouted as I drew closer to the portal.

"Fine. No one wanted you here anyway,"

Xavier yelled. "They wanted to leave you with Mab and do this journey with just me, but I told them to bring you. This is why. You're a spoiled brat."

I couldn't stop myself. It was all coming out, and I just couldn't stop. I snapped around to face him.

"Coming from the one that has everything handed to him on a golden platter. The one that had training at his disposal. The one who lived his life in the Summit. Yes, it must be so difficult to be you. Poor you. Your mother wanted to look for our brother instead of being around you. Well, guess what? I didn't have our mother, either. Damian didn't have our mother. And before we could even meet her, she was gone. And the ONLY person in this miserable universe that gave a damn about me is in the clutches of Alpha. My father, the one who does love me more than life itself. The one that selflessly has taken care of me for years. So, yes. I am *totally* the spoiled brat here. I'm the spoiled brat that has been left defenseless against ANYTHING! If you would take the silver spoon out of your mouth and stop pointing fingers at everyone, you just might see that."

My face was hot and red. Xavier's nostrils flared with anger. "Just go!" he demanded.

"Gladly, but one thing you must know before I do leave," I started as I turned back to the portal, not even sure how I knew what I was about to say. "All three of us must meet Starfire, or she won't help any of us. We all must be there. So good luck on your hunt for nothing."

I stepped through the portal and landed on a sandy beach. There was nothing but sand and water for miles. I turned around to find trees upon trees behind me. There was a huge mountaintop with a pillar of smoke coming from it. Someone must be here. Maybe they can help me hide out until the end of the world. Even as I thought the words, I just sat on the ground in defeat as tears began to bubble to the surface.

"Your father was right. You do have a temper," Damian said as he sat down on the ground beside me.

"What are you doing here?" I asked, swiping at the tears and wiping them from my face so he wouldn't see them.

"I couldn't let you wander off on your own. What kind of a protector do you think I am?" he asked, nudging me lightly with his arm.

"I was sure you would be tagging along with the others to who knows where," I replied.

"Right now, they're arguing about whether you were right with everything you said," he said. "You're right, at least I think so. They should have been training both of you, not just singling one out to be the greatest of all."

"They were most likely training him to kill you, and they knew I wouldn't," I replied.

"Fair enough, but still not fair to you," he remarked back. "I think you have a greater chance of taking me out than anyone."

"Oh, I do?" I asked with a choked laugh, still wiping the tears from my face that flowed relentlessly.

"Yes," he replied. "There's no way I could ever hurt you. Not to even protect myself." He wiped a straggling tear away.

We both stared at each other as that familiar feeling began to stir once more in my belly. I quickly stood from my seat on the ground and pointed off into the distance where I had seen the smoke wafting up.

"Who do you think that is?" I asked.

"Most likely Starfire," Gwendolyn replied. "I'm surprised you found the right portal. I would have taken us through so many different ones that it would have taken much longer to reach her. Impressive job."

She offered me a smile, an apologetic one. I nodded an affirmation of apology accepted. I watched as Xavier and Praeziel stepped through the portal as well. Xavier scowled at me and refused to acknowledge me after that point. So much for true love, eh? Damian snorted. Eavesdropping again, I see.

I can reply as well, but only to my favorite people, he replied in my head. I smiled and felt the tension melt from my shoulders.

"So, are you three ready to meet the game-changer?" Praeziel asked.

"As ready as I ever will be," I replied and began to head the group to the smoking mountain.

CHAPTER 3

WE HAD BEEN WALKING for hours and had come no closer to the base of the mountain than what we were when we landed on the beach. The sun beat down on us in the unforgiving, growing palm trees. I had nearly finished the canteen of water that I had filled from the river while in the Otherworld. We slogged on down the path we were following when we came across a boulder I knew for a fact we had already passed.

"We're going in circles," I said, dropping my gear to the ground and plopping down under the shade of a palm tree. "She must have some sort of glamour or force field up."

The rest of the group followed suit, dropping their gear to the ground and sitting down under some shade. I watched them pull their canteens from their bags and drink. I licked my parched lips and gave my canteen a small shake. It had maybe a sip or two left in it. I needed to save it for when I needed it. I stuck the canteen back into my bag when I felt a nudge. I looked over, and Damian was holding his canteen out for me to take a drink.

I shook my head in protest. "You're going to need it," I said, pushing it back toward him.

"Well, it won't do us much good if you die from dehydration," he replied, handing it back to me again.

I took the canteen from him, sighing, knowing that arguing would be futile. I took a swig and handed it back to him. He put the cap back on and placed it back in his bag. We all sat examining our surroundings until Xavier broke the silence with the question we were all thinking.

"So, what do we do now?" he asked. "We can't uncloak our wings, or else we would alert everyone to our location. We can't keep walking in this stupid circle, or we will drop off like flies."

He was right. We were stuck in a situation we had no way out of. As the chatter came for ideas, my gaze lingered on the path we had been on. I stared and stared until a glint of sunlight seemed to bounce off an imaginary wall. I blinked a few times to see if my eyes had been playing tricks on me. The glint was still there. I stood up and walked over to the area that had a slight light reflection to it. I could feel the energy buzzing from it. The hairs on my arms stood up when I got close to it, almost as if it were an electrical current. Dad had taught me how to pick up electrical fields when I was little. He didn't want me getting zapped by fences or walking straight into a power plant. I reached out to touch the wall and was zapped hard by whatever it was Starfire was using as a ward. I fell on my back, and the wind was knocked further out of my lungs.

"Luxina," I heard through a tunnel. There was a ringing in my ears, and all I could do was see the blurred faces over the top of me. I could hear nothing but loud bells. I couldn't even move.

"She isn't breathing," another voice garbled. Hands were on me, pressing my chest while someone else blew air into my lungs. "Stay with me!" I heard voices calling out. "Luxina!" The voices were desperate.

The sounds of the surrounding area came into focus, and I coughed, choked, and gasped for air.

Xavier and Damian knelt over me with bewildered faces. I continued to cough and gasp until I felt the air in my lungs become normal.

"What were you thinking?!" Xavier shouted at me.

"I saw the light hit a wall," I squeaked out as I sat up. Pain tore through my body. "What happened?" I asked groggily.

"You were electrocuted by whatever Starfire has up as a ward. You died!" Xavier shouted. "Don't ever do anything without checking with us. Next time, we might not be able to bring you back," he huffed and stalked off down the path.

"Don't wander too far," Praeziel called after him. "This could be a maze."

All he did was flick his hand to dismiss Praeziel and disappeared from view around the bend.

"I really didn't mean for that to happen," I stammered, apologizing. "I thought Starfire was just an oracle. How does she have magical wards up? Wards that electrocute you at that."

"She has to have the aid from warlocks," Gwendolyn replied as she wrapped my hand in a bandage.

I was confused as to why she was wrapping my hand when I glanced down. It was burned badly.

"The ward must react to any type of blood that isn't pure angelic," Praeziel offered as he saw the confusion on my face. "All three of you have the injections still swirling in your blood."

"Then, how do we even get to her?" Damian asked.

"I don't know. I wasn't expecting this at all," Praeziel replied. "We will rest here until we can come up with some sort of plan."

Damian nodded and looked at me as Gwendolyn finished the wraps on my hand. A faint memory of him and Xavier bent over me after Alpha gave me the injections came to mind.

"Get away from her," Xavier had said. *"She's my sister, too!"* echoed in my mind.

This time, however, they worked side by side to ensure that I was ok. In the haze I still felt from the electrocution, a very faint memory came to light. It was during one of our dreams Xavier and I had together when we met in the meadow. I remember running and tumbling through the flowers when I caught a glimpse of someone else who was there. But as fast as I saw the person, they vanished. All I remembered was red hair, curly red hair, peeking out from behind the tree in the middle of the meadow. Damian's eyes met mine, and they held a moment of vulnerability.

You were always there, weren't you? Watching us, making sure we were safe... I thought to him.

Yes, he replied, then stood, turned in the direction Xavier had gone, and followed him.

I wished my dad was here. He would know what to do right now. I sat helplessly and hopelessly, waiting for Damian and Xavier to return. I watched the force field shimmer as the sun set on the horizon. Fireflies began to emerge, and their floating lights made me miss my dad even more. We got our nicknames from Mother. She called him Firefly. He called me Firefly. Xavier and I called each other fireflies. There had to be more to the nickname, though. Fireflies didn't flit around with fire in their wake. And when we do use our powers, our eyes glow like the sun... like fireflies...

"Maybe..." I thought out loud instead of to myself.

"Maybe what?" Praeziel asked as he began to work on a fire for the night.

"Nothing. It's just a stupid afterthought," I replied.

"Maybe it is, maybe it isn't," he offered.

"We were called fireflies for nicknames because of our fire power. But what if that isn't the real reason for the nickname? We're the Shining Ones... we have to be able to harness the glow from the inside out without fire being used," I explained.

Praeziel stopped what he was doing and stared at me. "That might actually be the answer," he murmured, lost in thought.

"What might be the answer?" Xavier asked as he and Damian popped back up.

"Luxina, explain it to them," Praeziel stated and got up from the fire he was building. "I need to find Gwendolyn." As always, she had gone off to hunt for food.

"I was watching the fireflies' glow and thinking about our nicknames being fireflies. Whenever you two have used your powers, your eyes glow this bright golden color as if the sun were to burst through your eyes. We must be able to harness the power of our fire without bringing it forth and using it," I explained to Xavier and Damian.

They both took a seat beside me and mulled over what I had said. Xavier was the first to speak.

"How do we do that, though?" he asked.

"I have no idea," I replied, slumping and propping my chin on my hand.

"Yes, you do," Damian said quietly.

"What?" I asked, not understanding where he was going.

"Remember the apocalyptic nightmare you had the other day?" he asked.

I nodded.

"We were together in the dream, but we weren't close enough to save each other, right?" he asked.

"Right," I replied. And then the idea struck me. "We have to be together to activate it."

Damian offered his hands to both Xavier and me to hold. We each grabbed his hand and then grabbed each other's remaining hand. Energy erupted through us. This was far greater than the sensation I felt whenever I held Xavier's hand. This was something else. I could feel the energy jumping from Damian to Xavier and then to me and continuing around and around in a circle. Our bodies began to glow, and we were lifted from our seated position on the ground into the air as lights began to swirl around us like a twister. I looked at Damian and Xavier's faces and saw their eyes glowing as I had earlier in the day. Light orbs materialized from our kis and slowly moved toward the center of the circle we had created. They joined together, forming one large ball light that shot straight into the sky and exploded. The now dark island was lit up like the sun was up. The night became full day as the light show erupted into a full spectrum of colors swirling above. I felt the energy receding, and we slowly floated back to the ground and released one another's hands.

Praeziel came bounding up behind. "What was that?!" he shouted as Gwendolyn caught up to him.

"That was the Shining Ones," an unknown voice replied.

Our heads jerked in the direction we had heard the voice come from and saw a tiny, quaint woman standing there with a giant man at her side. She couldn't be but maybe five feet tall while her escort was at least seven feet. He towered over us, staring hard into our faces.

"Don't just stand there. That light show you just put on will alert every single creature that speaks, and word will get to Alpha where we are. Come now," she said and turned around to walk through the force field that had electrocuted me.

"Wait!" I started to shout and watched as she passed through it easily.

"The field is down," she said as if to answer my forming question. "Now, come along." She glanced at Praeziel and Gwendolyn. "All of you."

We followed her, and once we passed through the barrier that had been up, our eyes widened in surprise and awe. It was an oasis inside the barrier. The whole island was apparently a glamour. We could see for miles as we stood upon a cliff. There were waterfalls and jungles. A rainforest went on end throughout the valley that lay below us. Rainbows filled the sky as birds danced through the clouds.

"Where are we?" I asked, breathlessly taking in the sights.

"This place is called Lightshade. It's home to all warlocks," Starfire replied with a shimmering grin. "It never gets dark here. There is always sunshine to remind the warlocks that peace exists.

They weren't always privy to this place. Before they banded together to escape the clutches of the mortal world, they lived in darkness. The place they used to call home was nothing but an abyss. It was called Shadowmaw. Alpha had cursed them into hiding. When my family found them, they offered them an oasis away from people and Alpha, where they would never be found again. We took Sable Island and helped them put up a glamour so no one would be able to find the island on the seas again. From there, they built this paradise for their children to grow and learn what they can do with their magic."

"It's beautiful!" I breathed.

"Follow me, and I will show you where I live," Starfire stated as she began to lead us down a winding path from the cliff.

Exotic flowers I had never seen before bloomed on either side of the path and seemed to have a glow of their own as we traipsed down the hill following behind Starfire. Purples, pinks, and blue foliage lined the pathway, and it almost looked as if they reached out for us as we passed by.

"Will any of the plants here hurt us?" I asked as I examined the exotic breeds bending to touch us.

"No, unlike the plants and water in the Otherworld, nothing here is dangerous," Starfire replied. "A lot of these plants themselves possess magical powers that, when ingested, help aid the warlocks with their magic. Some are herbs that we use to treat illnesses or aid in magical workings. Then others are just for beauty." She stopped to smell some type of rose bush that was growing off to the right of the path. It had unusual color blooms on each stem that were colors I had never seen before. "Sometimes, you just need a little beauty in your life to remind you why you're important to the grand design."

As we walked, I continued to ask questions. "Did all the warlocks come here from Shadowmaw?"

A grim expression filled her face. "No, they did not. There were many that stayed behind. The idea of leaving behind their dark magic was too much for them to bear. So, they stayed," she replied sadly.

We rounded a bend, and there was a quaint cottage on the edge of the path that Starfire walked up to. She motioned for all of us to walk inside with her. From the looks on the outside, there was no way we would all fit in there comfortably, but once we stepped inside, we realized magic was still at work. Inside the cottage, it looked like a mansion. Rooms upon rooms were stacked with different things. She had a room full of magical books and another room that had a chemistry set constructed, most likely for making potions.

"And you're still just an oracle?" Xavier asked with a chuckle.

She shrugged her shoulders. "What can I say? I like to dabble in magic," she laughed. "I have plenty of rooms for you each to have your own instead of having to double up. There's plenty of food and water available in the kitchen and pantry. It has been a busy day, and I am sure you all are very tired after traveling as much as you have been. Pick a room and get rested. We have very little time to doddle. You have one more adventure to set forth on before I can begin to train you fully."

With that last comment, she retired to her own room and shut the door behind herself.

"Well, I don't know about all of you, but I am starving," Gwendolyn said as she started down the hall toward the kitchen.

We all rubbed our stomachs in agreement as they growled. My eyes scanned the rooms as we made our way down the long hall toward where Starfire kept her food. I was well-accustomed to a kitchen since I grew up mostly acting like a human child. Everyone began to pick through the pantry to find something to eat. She had everything you could dream of in there. Fresh vegetables, meat, dessert. My mouth salivated as I eyed a plate of macaroons. It had been so long since I had delighted in sugar that I nearly pushed people out of my way to get to the plate.

"You know sugar will kill you one day, right?" Damian asked, chuckling.

"Then, I will die happy," I replied as I stuffed two macaroons in my mouth at once. "Try one," I mumbled through the crumbs that escaped my lips as I talked with a full mouth.

"And I believe I lost my appetite," Xavier replied.

I made a face, and everyone laughed. We gorged ourselves sitting around a table merrily. Food was slim pickings while we had been journeying. It was mostly foraged berries, if there were any, and whatever we could find for meat. Starfire had pallets of berries, cheeses, loaves of bread, everything I missed while searching for her. We all cleaned up the mess we had made and headed up the stairs to find a room to crash in. A sudden panic overcame me as I realized this would be the first time in a year that I wouldn't have company right beside me in a circle around the fire. As Praeziel and Gwendolyn slipped off into the rooms they had chosen, I stopped Xavier as Damian entered a room at the end of the hall.

"Mind if we bunk together tonight?" I asked, not trying to sound too desperate.

He glanced between the bedroom he had chosen and me as if debating what he should do.

"Not tonight," he replied as he went to walk into his room.

"What did I do?" I asked, stepping closer to him. "If I said something or did something that was out of line or that offended you, please, just let me know. I don't like being locked out, and you have had me shut out for so long now…"

"I can't do this right now, Luxina," Xavier said, stepping further into the room.

"Why? Why are you shutting me out? What are you afraid of?" I demanded.

He was quiet for a moment before he answered, closing the door. "Every time we are close together, people die."

The door closed in my face, and I felt the tears welling behind my eyes with a knot of anxiety building in my chest. All the doors were shut with people behind them, not fearing things the way I did. I had never spent a day in my life alone. I always had my dad, and when I was taken, I had Xavier. And even when I didn't have him, I still had the comfort of having Praeziel and Gwendolyn around the circle with me. I walked numbly to the room in between Damian and Xavier and entered it, closing the door quietly behind me. I stared at the inviting bed that called to me to come and lie in it. I couldn't make it there, though. I slunk to the floor at the door, pulled my knees to my chest, and buried my head in my arms, rocking gently back and forth.

Was it true? Am I the reason everyone dies? Had it not been for Xavier taking me to Stygia, those who died or were captured would not have been put in that position had I not been taken there. Was our mother's death my fault as well? How many others have pledged their lives to keep us safe and out of harm's way? We have forged alliances with the fey and with the Watchers. We saw what happened to the Watchers. Would the same fate come to the Seelie and Unseelie courts for aiding us? Will there be no end to Alpha's revenge? How many people and creatures would have to die to stop this inevitable war?

I was too afraid to close my eyes alone. The memory of the nightmarish prophecy still echoed in my mind from the previous night. I sat underneath the window that was enchanted to filter in moonlight instead of the ever-shining sun outside. A light knock at the door jolted me from my thoughts. I stood and walked to the door, cracking it open. Damian stood on the other side with a sympathetic look in his eyes.

"Can't sleep?" he asked.

I shook my head and opened my door wider for him to walk in. "I don't ever want to sleep again," I replied, closing the door after him.

"I couldn't agree more with that statement," he said as he plopped on the bed.

Instead of sitting down beside him, I paced the floor as his eyes watched me go back and forth. A million different things ran through my tired mind. Questions of how we were going to pull this off and pull that off tugged and pulled at me until I was exasperated with everything. I was too anxious to sleep, and even though I was tired, my body wanted to do something else instead of sleep. I turned to Damian, who sat perched on the bed like a cat waiting for attention.

"Train me?" I asked, raising my eyebrow up. "There's no sleep in sight for me. Unless, of course, you want to sleep, then no worries."

He stood from the bed with a smile. "I thought you would never ask," he replied.

We opened the door, and I quietly waited outside of his room while he gathered some weapons from his bag. When he emerged and closed his door behind him, we tiptoed down the hall, made our way down the stairs, and bounded outside into the midday sun. We chose a spot in front of the cabin that had bare ground, so we didn't mess up any of the grass or plants and also in case someone came searching for us.

"Alright, what first?" I asked as I placed myself in front of him.

"Let's start with the basics first. Hand to hand combat," he replied. He held up his hands, palms facing outward. "I want you to punch my hands."

"Easy enough," I said.

I squared my body off and threw alternating jabs into his hands.

"Not bad," he said. "For a three-year-old." He laughed and ducked as I threw a punch at the side of his head. "You must anticipate your enemy. Have you ever played chess?" he asked.

"Yeah, Dad taught me when I was little," I replied. "How does that help in punching?"

"Hand to hand combat is like a chess game. You must plan for what your enemy will do five steps ahead of you. You must learn their maneuvers and use them against them. Swing at me again."

I did as instructed, and he blocked my arm with his hand.

"Now block mine," he said.

He swiped at me, and I mimicked the move he made, knocking his punch away before it could land anywhere.

"The best offense is a good defense," he said with a devilish grin. "Alright, I am going to hold my hands up again, and you're going to punch at them. I want two left jabs and one right."

I nodded. He held his hands up, and I delivered the two left jabs and the right jab.

"Again," he demanded.

I obliged. Two left jabs and a right.

"Again!" he demanded.

Two left jabs and a right.

He swiped his right hand out, and I ducked out of the punch.

"Again!" he demanded.

Soon, we fell into a rhythm. Two left jabs and a right, swoop, duck. By instinct, after I ducked, I lifted my leg and swung it around. He caught it in midair and chuckled.

"Can we hold off on throwing other body parts into this? We must get you mobile before we start the fun stuff." He grinned in delight. It looked as if teaching me really brought out the spirit that looked broken when he first arrived. "Ok, so next. We are going to Tango while you throw jabs. Jab, step; jab, step; jab, step, swoop, duck, then jab. Got it?"

"Uh-huh," I replied with a nod.

I jabbed with my left hand while stepping forward with my right foot, and he mimicked my steps. This time, he advanced toward me while I threw my jabs. We practiced this a few times until I was moving with grace.

"Faster!" he demanded.

We moved back and forth in the circle we had made. I would advance punching, and he would push back. He caught me by surprise and tossed out a punch I wasn't expecting. He caught me in the cheek with it. I didn't stop, though. I kept going, and the next time the surprise punch came,

I was ready and blocked it, delivering a blow of my own to him.

"Nice!" he exclaimed. "Now, you can throw in those legs."

We quickened our pace with the jabs, ducks, feet moving, legs kicking. I was having fun. Why hadn't anyone done this with me before?

"They looked at you like a girl that needed protection as opposed to an angel warrior like you are," he replied.

"Well, they should know better," I said, still jabbing and moving. "What did they expect me to do? Sit by all pretty-like on the sidelines, hoping no one came my way?"

"Pretty much," he replied with a small shrug of the shoulders. "I mean, they had the best intentions at heart. They just wanted to keep you safe. A promise that Praeziel made to Incaendiel."

"What's next?" I asked.

"Ready to learn backflips?" he asked in reply, stripping his shirt off.

"Um," I was able to get out when he lifted off in the air, sailing backward, and landed steadily on his feet.

His skin glistened in the sun as sweat beaded along his torso. That was clearly a distraction to me. I shook my head a bit to get my mind back in training. Instead of a back tuck like he did, I did a standing back handspring back tuck. He cocked his head to the side in confusion.

"I did gymnastics at one of the schools," I replied with a proud smile.

"You're just FULL of surprises, aren't you?" he asked, a stealthy grin spreading. "Alright, utilize everything they taught you in gymnastics. Cartwheels, back tucks, back springs, all of it. Don't forget to keep your feet moving, jab, parry, block, and duck."

"Got it, teach," I replied, throwing a jab his way.

We moved around the circle, almost as if we were dancing. The moves were so rhythmic and methodical. I could read his body language and ascertain what his next move would be to appropriate my next move.

"You were right," I said, a bit breathless. "It is like a game of chess."

I threw a punch, and he ducked down, kicking out his leg and spinning it toward me. I jumped over it and did a backflip out of the way. He was on me no sooner than my feet hit the ground, and I ducked out of the way of his swooping arm. I spun my leg around and caught his legs, knocking him from his feet. He didn't land on his back, though. Instead, he barrel-rolled into a crouch. We ran at each other, throwing jabs, parrying, ducking, neither one of us landing any hits.

"Oh, I enjoy this," he remarked, swinging his leg at me as I tucked and rolled, kicking out with my leg.

"This is so exhilarating!" I exclaimed.

"Of course, it is. It's in your blood," he replied.

He picked up two of the small pen-like things he had when he fought the werewolves. He clicked a button, and they burst into swords.

"Ready for some weapons training?" he asked.

"I thought you would never ask," I replied with a laugh.

He walked the sword over and handed it to me.

"Sword fighting is terribly like hand-to-hand combat with the exception you are using an object and not your hands. So, you throw the sword the way you would your hands. You use the sword to parry as you did with your hands. And of course, duck."

I nodded in acknowledgment. He brought his sword up with both hands on the hilt. I positioned my hands the same way.

"Now, swing your sword at me," he stated.

I did as I was told and swung the sword around, bringing it down over my head at him. He parried the sword with his.

"Nice form!" he praised. "Now, again. Except this time, come from the other side. It will be left, right, left just like with your jabs."

I planted my feet firmly apart and swung the sword the same exact way but in the opposite direction, and it landed neatly on his parrying sword. I repeated. My moves became faster, and soon our feet were moving the same way we had during the hand-to-hand combat.

"Do you have two smaller ones?" I asked. "This one is large and tires me out really quickly. Maybe two smaller ones I could move with agility."

He lifted two of the pens from his pocket and handed them to me. He clicked the button on the side of the sword, and it capsized back down into the pen-sized instrument it had been. I clicked the buttons on the sides of the ones he handed me, and two medium-sized swords appeared. I balanced the weight of each in my hands.

"These feel much better," I said, testing them in the air.

"It's because you're a double hander," he replied.

"What's that?" I asked.

"You work better with a weapon in each hand."

I lifted the swords in my hand and leapt toward him. I came down on his sword, and he pushed me back and then proceeded to bombard me with his sword. I worked my blades smoothly and carelessly, getting swifter as I parried his attack. He ducked down and swooped his leg that I jumped over. We continued. I moved my hands like I was painting the sky. I would duck, weave, bombard, parry, and repeat.

We each took a step back and clicked the swords back into place. I went to hand the swords back to him when he raised his hand, shaking it.

"Keep them. You earned them," he said breathlessly. "I haven't had a sparring buddy in a while, and you best even the greater demons. I was putting in effort in that last five minutes."

"Well, thank you… I think." I grinned in satisfaction. "Now, what about my powers? Can you teach me to hone them?"

He walked over to me and turned me around to face the opposite direction. He put one hand on my stomach and his other hand on my arm.

"You feel it from there," he said in my ear, shivers erupting over my body. "But instead of letting it burst through your whole body, you channel the flames to here," he said, running his hand down my arm to my fingertips.

My heart raced as his light touch stopped on my hand. His voice was light and sweet, caring.

"Give it a try," he whispered.

I felt the burn in my stomach and felt the heat rise from my skin. "What if I hurt you?" I whispered in return.

"You can't hurt me," he replied as his hands cooled to freezing temperatures.

My heat ran up through my chest, through my arm, and out of my fingers. A torch of fire sprayed from my hand, and I panicked. I didn't know how to stop.

"Now, bring it back gently," he whispered.

I pulled the fire back in the way Praeziel had shown me and stopped when the flames reached my hand. He ran his cold hand through the fire before I could protest.

"See," he said. "You can't hurt me."

I watched as his hand danced in the ball of fire in my hand. I glanced out of the corner of my eye at his face. It was so intent, but yet so serene. He turned toward me and caught my eye. We were caught in a gaze for just a moment before he broke it. He dropped his hands from my body as the fire disappeared in my hands.

"Well, you passed the training. I would give you a card, but I'm fresh out," he chided.

"She did more than pass training," Starfire said, walking out of her door. "She learned what her blood was meant to do. The power that rests inside all of you is so much more than just fire and ice." She gazed at me hard. "Would you like to spar with a few of my men? Show them what you learned? They won't take it easy on you."

I saw a flash of irritation cross Damian's face. Was he jealous?

"Sure," I replied. "Will they be using magic?"

"Of course," she replied with a grin.

She snapped her fingers, and a young man materialized in front of me. He was about my age. He was olive-skinned, with dark cat-like eyes. His hair was spiked with metallic green. He wielded two swords in his hands. I brought my swords out and clicked the buttons. He grinned at me when his swords burst into a purple glow. That must be the magic he uses. I readied myself when he made the first move. His blades sliced through the air like butter as I parried and blocked his attacks. I methodically moved around as Damian had taught me. One of his blades nicked my arm, and red bubbled to the surface of my skin.

"Oh, you shouldn't have done that," I said coolly.

I watched his eyes widen in surprise with a hint of fear. I pulled the heat through my body the way Damian had shown me. Except when it got to my hands, I funneled it into my swords. They burst into flames on the blades, and I advanced on my target. I swiped through the air faster and faster, backing him into a corner. I pointed the blades at his throat until he dropped his swords in defeat.

"Now THAT was awesome," Xavier said, breaking the silence of the fight.

I shook the young man's hand before he disappeared as quickly as he had appeared. I walked back over to Starfire, snuffing the fire out on my swords before putting them away.

"Now, you are ready, Shining One," Starfire said with a grin. "Are you ready for the quest?"

She looked around at Damian and Xavier, and then her eyes rested on me.

"Yes," we all said in unison.

"Good, because only you three will be able to go," she replied. "Praeziel and Gwendolyn cannot go where you have to go."

Praeziel and Gwendolyn stood off on the porch with solemn faces.

"We thought it would be best if she told you," Praeziel said.

"Where are we going?" I asked quizzically.

She smiled deeply. "Why, my dear, you're going to Atlantis."

CHAPTER 4

Damian, Xavier, and I geared up for our journey. Xavier and Damian pilfered through the weapons available to take. Damian grabbed his sword, a bow and arrow quiver, and a mace that he strapped to his back. Xavier picked up a sword, a throwing axe, and some ninja stars that worked as boomerangs. I had the swords that Damian gave me. As we packed to leave, the young man I had sparred against appeared within the cottage and bowed to me.

"I want you to take my blades," he said.

He held out the two hand knives that he hadn't used earlier. I examined them closely and saw they wrapped around your hand as brass knuckles would and that the blade curved on the outside of your hand. I picked them up from his hands, and they immediately sprouted the purple haze that he had used. I smiled in appreciation.

"Thank you," I said. "What's your name?"

"My name, I do not know. I was just a baby when I came to the island with Starfire. My parents stayed behind in Shadowmaw. The name Starfire gave me is Reilak. My parents were necromancers, so the name fits," he replied.

"Thank you, Reilak." I bowed my head in appreciation, and he stepped away to stand beside Starfire.

I placed the hand knives around my palms and fitted them over the top of my hands. They were snug like gloves, almost as if they were made specifically for me. Starfire walked around and handed us each a red hat. I frowned, staring at what she gave us.

"What are these?" I asked.

"They're called red caps. They are what merfolk use to swim and breathe in the water. Merfolk are not like mermaids. They actually live quite like humans except at the bottom of the ocean in a bubble-type fortress," she explained. "This is how you will swim to Atlantis. Don't put it on until you are ready to dive into the water, or else you will drown above ground. It gives you gills."

I tucked the cap into the back of my pants. She had given us all new clothes to wear. I wasn't enthused when she handed me an outfit that was leather. When I put it on, it grabbed my body in all the places I had never shown off before. My breasts were noticeable as well as my butt. The top was too short, and my belly button showed. No matter how I tugged it down or my pants up, neither covered that area, and it made me feel a tiny bit insecure.

"What are we looking for?" Damian asked.

"Once you get to the city of Atlantis, you will come to a dome that surrounds the city underwater. You must hold hands to walk through the dome. On the inside, remove the red caps as there won't be water but rather air for you to breathe. Hidden within the grand city is a chalice that has a white powder in it. Put the chalice in this bag," she said, handing us a satchel. "This material is specifically woven to shrink around the contents it holds, making an airtight seal. Water will not get in the chalice, and the contents will not spill out. When you get to the surface, blow on this," she said, handing over a seashell. "It will alert me to send the portal to bring you back."

"That seems easy enough," Xavier replied, taking the shell from her hand.

She looked at him gravely. "Be careful and mindful of whatever you encounter below the waters. The seas are filled with all kinds of creatures that mean to do you harm, mermaids especially. Since the sinking of Atlantis, they have claimed the place as their own. Mermaids were created by Alpha and are not the fairytale creatures you think them to be. If you must, kill them to escape."

All three of us exchanged glances and nodded in unison.

"Alright, Reilak. Make the portal," Starfire stated.

The young boy did a magical dance with his hands as they began to glow the same color purple the knives had been imbued with. He began to circle them around and around, and a translucent whirlwind circle appeared. We gazed through it, amazed. Unlike the faery portals that didn't show what was on the side, this portal showed us exactly where we would be stepping foot. There was rocky ground with waves crashing against it.

"Step through the portal, put on your red caps, and dive deep. Use this," she said, handing us each a necklace with a bright-colored stone on it. "These are special faery amulets and will glow in the dark."

We tied the necklaces around our necks and stepped through the portal. It disappeared behind us, and we found ourselves on a rocky beach area. Off in the distance, we could see a sailboat that I could only assume was used for fishing.

"Where exactly are we?" Xavier asked.

"Somewhere in the Mediterranean near Greece," Damian replied. "Don't you two read mythologies?"

"Yes," I replied. "We also know that the lost city of Atlantis was inhabited by a superior alien race created by older gods than Alpha."

"I see you listened intently when Sophia explained everything to you," he said, smirking. He fished his red cap out of the back of his pants. "You two ready? I don't like being out in the open and exposed like this."

Xavier and I grabbed our red caps from our pants as well, and we all put them on at the same time and then dived into the crashing waves. We began to sink when a slight panic took over me. I didn't know if the red caps were working yet or not, and I refused to drag in a breath of air under the water.

"Luxina, breathe!" Damian exclaimed through the underwater current.

I gulped in seawater and realized to my embarrassment that the red caps were indeed working properly.

"We can talk underwater?" I asked.

"It's all part of the enchantment on the red caps," Damian explained. "Let's go."

We swam, descending deeper and deeper into the ocean waters. The deeper we went, the less I could see the sun shining through the water. When darkness was just about to envelop us, the stones around our necks began to shine a bright, luminescent light. Each of our lights was a different color based on the color of the stone she had handed us. As soon as the dark depths were illuminated with our lights, and we could see again, there were behemoth creatures all around us that made strange noises under the water.

"They're whales," Damian explained. "They won't hurt us."

We swam alongside the massive creatures as they wailed in their language, talking to one another. We swam atop a large underground garden that had flowers with floating petals, long strings of grass, and colorful rocks that glowed like our necklaces.

"It's called a reef. The rocks are called corrals. The flowers are called sea anemones, and the grass is called seaweed. All these things are living creatures," Damian said.

I watched an orange and white fish pop out of what he called a sea anemone and float back in. It kept repeating the action before it came completely out and swam off along with the other creatures among the reefs. I saw things shaped like stars and pointy little round balls.

"Those are called urchins. Don't touch them. They're poisonous," Damian warned. "The other is called a starfish." He pointed to a little creature that looked like a mixed dragon-horse. "That's called a seahorse."

"How do you know all this?" I asked in wonder.

"I read a lot in my spare time," he replied.

Under the sea was a whole other world of enchantment, almost as if it existed apart from the mortal world. All kinds of sea creatures swirled around together, swimming absentmindedly as we passed by. It was just as breathtaking as when Starfire brought us to Lightshade. As we swam, the creatures took note of us and watched us curiously. A tiny little thing swam up to me and stayed beside me as we descended deeper into the water. It was followed by another and then another. Soon, I was surrounded by these teeny, little creatures. They looked a bit like fish, but they had faces.

"Damian, what are these?" I asked a bit nervously as more and more began to show up and circle me as we swam.

No sooner had I asked him than they all bared nasty, sharp little fangs.

"Luxina, swim as fast as you can away from them!" Damian shouted. "They're baby mermaids."

I picked up my speed, and the little creatures nipped and bit at my feet. I pushed myself harder as we all tried to outswim the bloodthirsty things. I felt my hand tugged and noticed Damian had grabbed hold of it and was pulling me faster away from the cloud of mermaids as they viciously snapped and bit, trying to mangle my feet.

"We must be getting close to the underwater kingdom," Damian said. "We have to be on the lookout. There will be all kinds of monsters protecting the entrance."

"If those are baby mermaids, where are the parents?" Xavier asked nervously.

"Let's hope we don't find out," Damian replied. "Mermaids are nastier than Starfire let on. It's why she said if we have to, kill them. They were made from the blood of Seelies and the venom of vampires, then mixed with demon blood. They are vile things and will eat you alive."

"I thought those were called sirens?" I asked as we gained momentum through the waters, catching a natural current.

"Sirens are far worse," Damian replied. "They sing you a song to lull you into sleep and then devour your body as you lay there, helplessly locked in a sweet nightmare."

We topped over a bank of tall seaweed when a glow deep in the water caught my eye.

"Is that?" I began to ask.

"Atlantis," Damian finished. "It's so deep down that no human would ever be able to find it."

As we grew closer to the glowing light, a creepy feeling came over me as if we were being watched. It was the kind of feeling that made my hair stand on end. The water buzzed with an energy unlike any I had ever felt.

"Do you two feel that?" I asked as we grew closer to the kingdom.

"Yes," Xavier replied, looking around in the darkness.

"I don't like this," Damian replied. "This feels off."

We continued to swim, expecting the light to grow bigger, but it was almost as if no matter how fast or hard we swam, the light still remained a reasonable distance off. We slowed our underwater pace and began to take note of our surroundings. There wasn't a single fish or creature that we could see. It was a dead wasteland under here.

"I don't like this at all," Damian repeated.

"Yeah, you said that," Xavier replied nervously. "Woah! Did you see that?"

"See what?" Damian asked, looking around nervously.

"It looked like some huge blanket of darkness that passed by on my left," he replied. "There it is again!" he shouted, pointing to the right of me.

Damian and I caught a glimpse of it. Damian readied his sword, and Xavier and I followed suit.

"What is that thing?" I asked, looking nervously all around me.

"I don't know, but I'm sure it thinks we are dinner," Damian replied slowly edging forward.

I caught whatever it was on my right when Xaiver and Damian yelled at the same time, "It's on my left."

"It can't be. I just saw it on my right," I protested.

We drew closer to the light, and the water around us fell dead silent. There wasn't an air bubble, a ripple, or a current. Damian motioned to his lips with his finger for us to be quiet.

No more talking. Use your thought speech, he commanded.

Ok, I replied.

No argument from me, Xavier said.

In the beginning, Alpha created night and day. He created land and sea, Damian began.

Yeah, we know the creation story, Xavier interrupted.

And in the sea, Damian continued, *held a behemoth that no man could ever survive. He had slain*

the great god of the abyss, Tiamat, and cast her into the
sea, creating what scriptures called Leviathan.

No sooner had he uttered the name from the scriptures than a howl erupted through the waters. A tentacle ripped through the water as we all scrambled to dodge the assault the beast began to commence. I watched as Damian parried with his sword, but I couldn't bring myself to hurt the poor creature that Alpha had created. Blood soaked through the seawater as they chopped and hacked the tentacles that flew to them, trying to grab them unsuspecting. As I stood watching the boys fight off the tentacles with their weapons, I hadn't realized that one of them was wrapped around my foot. It gave a hard jerk, and I was lifted off through the water.

"Do you think you are worthy of the treasure that lies in wait at Atlantis, you puny little angel?" it bellowed.

"Tiamat, wife of Drac?" I asked.

The leviathan stopped the assault, and the boys swam up to me and grabbed hold of my hands, pulling me from the grip the tentacle had on me.

"You know who I am?" she asked.

"At first, no. I just knew you were Leviathan until I ran the first name Damian had called you. Tiamat. I remember the story when Alpha created the heavens and the earth. When he created all his angels, the universe began to cave in on itself. He went to the Elder Gods to seek an answer. He came to you. He didn't like your answer but did it anyway. When it failed his power trip, he punished you. He stole you away from your own universe that toppled without you. The universe that was already growing old and dying that you were sustaining. He took you away before you could get all your creations off to safety. Those that were led to safety hid in plain sight here in Atlantis. You continue to protect your people from Alpha. Do you want your revenge? Help us!" I called.

"Who are you?" Tiamat asked, slithering through the water closer to me. "You're like angels, but not. Your blood runs thick with fire and ice."

"We are the Shining Ones," I replied. "The ones you helped create, so in extension, we are your people."

"Ah," she replied with a smile to her voice. "You are Sophie and Incaendiel's children." She looked at Damian. "Except you. You are only half-blood. Sophie's son, I presume?" she asked.

"Yes," he replied.

"What do you seek in Atlantis?" she asked.

"The chalice," Xavier replied. "We were sent by the Oracle Starfire to retrieve it. It's to complete our disenchantment."

"Yes, the enchantment," Tiamat mused. "I told Omega when she made Sophie and Incaendiel to give them all the power and not to hide it. It would have saved a lot of devastation and pain had she done what I said. She feared Alpha would destroy them, so she hid what they were."

"Will you let us pass? So, we can forever take down Alpha and put an end to his reign?" I asked.

"Do you understand what you are getting from Atlantis?" Tiamat asked.

"Just that it's a chalice full of a white powdery substance," Xavier replied.

"It's called manna," Tiamat replied. "A gift from the universe, if you wish to call it something. It is what molded us gods into being. Crafted from the molten lava of the brightest star and doused in the white powder, we were forged."

"Then, how does it help us?" I asked. "Won't that make us…"

"A god?" Tiamat finished my sentence. "Of course, my dear. What did you think you were? Just super angels? Omega made herself tiny little gods to take over once her and Alpha's rule ended. Sophie and Incaendiel were to be the new reigning superiors. They are far more powerful than Omega and Alpha combined. The power within you all is as deep and true as the power of all the remaining elder gods."

"So, you will let us pass?" Damian asked.

"I will let you pass on one condition," Tiamat began. "You are to swear to me that you will do whatever it takes to stop Alpha and bring an end to his rule. When he is dethroned, I may return to my abode."

"We want nothing more than to make Alpha pay for everything he has done to ruin this universe," I replied. "We would be more than happy to restore you to the cosmos."

"Then, you may pass, but I must warn you. The water only gets more treacherous past me. Creatures that have no thoughts live here, and they want nothing but one thing: to eat."

Tiamat moved aside so we could continue on our journey.

"Be careful, young Shining Ones. You are the future, and without you, there is no future."

We nodded to her in appreciation and continued past her to our destination, which seemed to grow no closer the further we swam. Her warning echoed in our minds, and we advanced with caution through the treacherous waters. We had no idea what to expect that laid in wait for us. Damian scoured the waters as we swam along with his weapons in hand.

"Luxina, arm yourself with the dueling swords I gave you," he ordered.

I reached to my sides, unhooked the swords from their sheaths, and clicked the activate buttons. The blades blazed under the water to their natural size, but I still had no idea why these would be better than the hand blades that Reikal had given me.

"The weapons I gave you were a gift from the Dark Queen Mab. She took my regular battle blades and turned them into weapons that specifically fought creatures with Seelie blood. They are made from iron and silver," he explained.

"When did you see the Dark Queen?" Xavier asked.

"After my escape from Alpha, I was unable to come directly to you. He had created monsters that followed me from his fortress. Terrifying things that he made me battle. Incaendiel saved me from certain death, and after fighting them for so long while running, the Dark Queen took me to the Otherworld with her. However, it was just a moment of respite. Those things followed me there. I spent quite a while battling through the Nightmares and Shadows realm," he explained.

"That's why you had the dust in your bag and knew what to do when I was attacked," I said. "Why didn't you tell us?"

"There was no time to fill you in completely on my adventures," Damian replied. "There's still so much more that I need to tell you both, but it can wait until after we get what Starfire needs us to acquire."

"What happened to the Otherworld people?" I asked. "Gwendolyn has been preoccupied for some time and not telling us what is bothering her."

"When we get back, I will tell you the whole story. We need to stay focused on this mission," he replied.

I nodded my okay, and we continued to swim through the dark depths. We came to the end of the bottom of the ocean, and it dropped off into some sort of ravine-type trench. Damian motioned for us to look. We followed his gaze, and in the middle of the trench, the great city of Atlantis stood with a grand dome encasing it.

"Look closely," Damian said as he took a knee, watching the waters.

We all looked intently at the waters surrounding the bright light emitted from Atlantis. It had things swimming around the kingdom as if they were protecting it. As we looked closer, we could see the creatures a bit better. The bottom half of their body was a fishtail, and the top half looked almost human.

"Mermaids," I murmured. "Why don't they look like the babies we came across? These… they look absolutely beautiful."

"If you were creating a monster that was deadly, would you want those unsuspecting of its deviant nature to be afraid of it and run away before it had a chance to tear the flesh from their body? Or would you rather they look majestically beautiful, lure those unsuspecting in, and then tear them to shreds?" Damian asked. "Alpha is a grand chess player. When you think you are five steps ahead of him, he is really ten steps ahead of you."

"So, what do we do? There is no way we can slip in undetected. There are too many of them swimming around," I asked.

"We fight our way through," Xavier replied, readying the sword in his hand.

"I don't think I am ready for that," I stammered, gulping down my welling anxiety.

"You will do fine," Damian replied. "Just do what you were doing with me."

I looked to my swords, unsure of myself, with Damian's words echoing in my mind to reassure me. He motioned for us to follow him, and we began our descent into the trench. We tucked our lights beneath our shirts as we grew closer to Atlantis so we didn't alert the mermaids of our approach. We swam through banks of seaweed to hide our approach to the gates of Atlantis. A sudden jerk brought my attention from watching the circling mermaids to the seaweed we were swimming in. My foot had gotten tangled up in the tall strands of the underwater grass. I worked my fingers against the blade, trying to release myself, but the more I struggled with the vine-like grip it had on me, the tighter the tendrils grew.

"Damian, is seaweed a live creature, too?" I whispered as I struggled to untangle myself.

My finger slipped, and the side of seaweed cut me like paper would slice through a finger. It grew tighter around my ankle, cutting it, and another piece grabbed my other leg. I picked up my swords from the bank side, and a tendril snaked over and grabbed me by the wrist. Damian and Xavier were paying me no mind while they waited for me to get untangled, keeping watch with their backs to me.

"A little help, please?" I squeaked as another blade shot out and grabbed me by the torso.

It was as if they couldn't hear me talking. They floated there with their backs turned to me, not speaking nor moving, just watching. The seaweed clenched tighter around me as more and more blades grabbed my body. The tendrils tightened and cut through the clothing. I began to feel myself being pulled closer and closer into the dark roots of the plants. My bones felt like they were being crushed like a snake eating its prey.

"Help!" I screamed louder than I intended.

Damian and Xavier whipped around; however, the two figures that now stood before me were neither of them. They were mermen. They smiled at me, and terror flooded my body as I counted each sharp tooth that was in their mouths.

"Damian! Xavier!" I shouted, struggling against the iron grip I was held in.

More seaweed snaked around my body and began to cover my face.

"The perfect dinner for us tonight, is it not?" one of the mermen asked the other.

"Oh yes, seaweed with a side of angel. Perfectly delectable," he mused.

Just as the seaweed began to cover my eyes, I watched swords slice through their midsections, cutting them neatly in half. Xavier and Damian stood before me with cuts and scrapes of their own. Their blades worked at the seaweed, hacking me from its briny grips. I gasped for air as the blade that had wrapped around my neck, strangling me, released. I clamored from the shallow grave I had nearly found myself in sushi-style.

"Stay out of the seaweed," Damian muttered.

"You don't have to tell me twice," I replied, equally annoyed. "I thought I was surely a goner. I thought you both were still right here with me. What happened?"

"The seaweed grabbed us like you and dragged us down the trench. Our powers are useless under the water," Xavier replied, slicing the final tendril from my leg.

Deep gashes were left behind from where vines had gripped me so hard. Damian inspected them as Xavier stood to watch for other mermaids or mermen to swim by.

"As soon as we get to dry land, we need to get something on that and bandage it," Damian stated. "What worries me is the scent of blood in the water now. We will be swarmed if we don't hurry."

I nodded, and we swam past the seaweed beds, making sure not to get tangled in them anymore. The wound around my ankle was the worst and stung in the seawater. The pain began to grow to an unbearable stabbing feeling. I looked down at my ankle to see if there was poison or something leaching from it, causing the increasing pain. Hundreds of little baby mermaids swarmed my leg, biting at it like little, tiny piranhas. I screamed out in pain as they bit and dragged their teeth across the wounds. Their mouths were too small to tear much skin. Damian and Xavier swam to my side, swiping at the creatures with their swords, but they were too tiny to do any real damage to them.

"There's too many of them," Xavier remarked as they started swarming him and Damian as well.

I didn't wait to argue about whether our powers worked here or not. I grabbed Xavier's hand with a shattering exertion of power as we touched. I built a fire from my belly, and the water began to boil around me. The boil extended a ten-foot radius, killing any and all those little monsters that swam to us. Within minutes, they had all been boiled away, floating from the depths and upwards.

"We were told to use our power together, and this is why," I stated, examining the damage that was done to my leg and ankle.

"We have problems," Damian muttered.

I followed his gaze and looked around the tiny cavern we were floating in front of. Mermaids by the thousands hissed and snarled at us. We had killed their babies, and they were enraged about it. Damian and Xavier grabbed my hands, and we began to swim as fast as we could through the waters as thousands of mermaids swarmed at us. Pure white light enveloped us as our powers as the Shining Ones burst forth. The mermaids kept their distance, still trying to rip us to shreds, but the light was so bright it burned their skin. We swam at speeds I had never gone with more and more mermaids coming at us, attracted, and yet repulsed by the bright light we emitted. They knew what we were, and they wanted to get their hands on us and feast upon our special blood. We barreled through the water at warp speed with the light of Atlantis growing closer and closer. The sea all around us blackened with the bodies of the mermaids that reached out to grab us, retreating their hands as they burned off in the pure white light.

We were almost to the dome when another sea creature swooped in and knocked us apart. Damian and Xavier were more than twenty yards away from me and from each other as well as we tried to come to our senses from the blow. A massive serpent rose to our left and had nine heads.

"What is that?" I asked in alarm, trying to swim to Damian.

A tentacle came down in front of me, blocking my way as I scrambled quickly backward.

"It's the Lernaean Hydra," Damian called out from the other side.

Another tentacle careened down at me as I swam out of its reach, just as it smacked into the ground. I tried making my way to Xavier, but another arm reached out, slamming me to the ground and blocking me. I was trapped by the monster. Arm after arm swooped down around me as I dodged the assault. Behind me waited a barrage of mermaids to rip my flesh from my bones. There was no escape.

The hand knives that Reikal had given me began to glow a bright purplish color. My hands began to move as if controlled by another person. They danced the way Reikal's did when he summoned a portal for Starfire. The water began to swirl around me like a whirlpool. It began to recede around me as the whirlpool grew larger and larger, driving the hydra back from me. The mermaids screeched in anger as they were pushed back away from me, and Damian and Xavier were exposed to the center with me.

"How did you do that?" Damian asked, removing his red cap to breathe.

Xavier followed Damian's lead and removed his red cap, then pulled the one from my head as well.

"I'm not the one doing it," I replied, motioning with my head toward my hands, which were still dancing.

"Will it move with you?" Xavier asked.

I shrugged my shoulders. "It's worth a shot." I began to walk forward as my hands continued to glide and dance through the air. The water kept receding and would fall in behind us as we walked closer to the dome covering Atlantis. We stood before the entrance as I continued to push the water away from us.

"Grab onto my arms and then run," I instructed.

They did as I said, and we ran full force to the dome as the water began to crash down behind us. We were just at the gates when the water pushed us, and we all tumbled as one through the dome that opened and shut quickly, trapping the water outside of it.

Xavier handed me my red cap, which, oddly enough, was completely dry. I stuffed the cap into the back of my pants, and we all surveyed our surroundings. We were standing on a massive land bridge that looked like it stretched at least half a mile across various motes. The city was a huge circle broken into smaller circles the closer you got to the center. The architectural structures were remarkably similar to the old pillar-style Colosseum in Italy and the architecture of ancient standing buildings in Greece. Two-story buildings jutted out on their own little bridges, creating a tapestry of circular patterns around the center of the city. The streets were inlaid with golden bricks, and statues that appeared to be Greek figures stood along the sides of the streets. It was like glancing at history that had been frozen in time. The city sparkled and glowed underneath the glowing light that hung above the centermost point of the area.

"Textbooks say that the Atlanteans were able to find a power source that wasn't electrical in any fashion to power their cities and hover vehicles," Damian explained as our eyes looked over the marvels of the lost and hidden place.

"They were an advanced civilization is why," I replied. "They came from outer space and lived in a galaxy far from this one. Tiamat was their Goddess."

We walked the empty streets looking for some sign of life, but if there was any, they were hidden away in their homes, away from the windows. The place was a ghost town, even though Tiamat acknowledged that her people were safely tucked away inside the walls of the dome. As we drew closer to the large building at the center of the ancient civilization, a hum could be heard in the air.

"That's the sound of whatever energy they are using to keep this place running," I said, looking for electrical wires. "My only guess is the inlaid gold along the roads is what helps push the electrical current throughout the city like ley lines."

"Did Starfire give any indication where this chalice was supposed to be stowed away here?" Xavier asked. "I mean, we're just walking in a straight line to a place that could probably kill us with electrical currents."

"I believe, if I am not mistaken, that is the inner city, and that is exactly where we need to be," Damian replied.

"I hope you're right," Xavier mumbled as we drew closer to the large, round building.

As we made it to the center of the city, outside of the large dome building was a magnificent landscape. It had growing foliage, flowers, fruit trees, olive trees, nut trees, and so much more. At the very center of the garden, there was a fountain that had an angel in the center of it. The guys swept by me as I stopped to admire the statue. The angel held a sword in one hand and a chalice in the other. I looked closer at the cup, squinting to make sure I saw things correctly. Is that…

"Guys, I think I found it," I said as tons of soldiers swarmed the courtyard we stood in. Damian and Xavier ran back to where I stood, and we faced off against the warriors as they pointed their swords and spears at us.

"Who dares disturb the peace and tranquility of our sunken city?" a voice called out over the crowd of soldiers.

A man and woman emerged as the soldiers stepped aside to let them through.

"What do you want?" the woman asked, narrowing her eyes at us.

Of course, we didn't look peaceful strapped to the gills with weapons.

"We were sent here by the Oracle to retrieve the chalice," I replied, motioning to the cup that the angel held.

"And what makes you think that it belongs to anyone other than our city that you so dare to breach our gates and try to steal it?" she asked in reply.

"We need it," Damian replied. "Tiamat gave us her blessing to retrieve it."

"Ah, you mean the Leviathan that stands guard for our city. Tiamat is no more than a cast aside goddess slew by the god of this galaxy, quickly gaining power he never had in the beginning. She is a moot existence," the woman replied. "So, I ask you again, angels, what gives you the right to take what isn't yours?"

The soldiers took a step closer to us, pointing their weapons even closer at us.

"Because it is as much ours as it is yours," I replied heatedly. "We were forged from the dying sun of your universe. The manna in that cup will bring us to full power to save the universe from the god you so callously speak of who slew your goddess."

"I don't believe you," she replied. "Guards! Dispatch the thieves and toss their dead bodies to the mermaids."

Just as the soldiers stepped another step closer to us, I grabbed Damian and Xavier's hands and willed with all my might for the fire to sprout faster than it usually did. Instead, the bright light shot from our bodies as we rose into the air. The faces of the soldiers contorted into fear, as did their leader's face. They hit their knees and laid their foreheads against the ground.

"We plead for your mercy," the leader begged without lifting her forehead from the ground. "We were brash and mistaken in our bad judgment. We beg for mercy from the Council of El. Take the cup. Take anything that you desire, oh Shining Ones."

We descended to the ground below and released our hands. The Atlanteans remained in their positions, afraid to look at us.

"We do not wish to hurt you," I said, kneeling before the leader and offering her my hand.

She lifted her head slightly from the ground to see my outstretched hand. She took my hand, and I lifted her to a standing position.

"Again, apologies, your majestic grace," she said, bowing her head. "We have protected the chalice for many years for the prophetic ones to come and lay claim to it. I had no idea that they would be young ones."

"Prophetic ones?" Xavier asked.

"Yes!" she exclaimed. "Prophecy spoke of the grand emergence of three Shining Ones to bring the evil of the universe to its knees." She glanced from my face to Xavier's face. "Has no one told you about the prophecy?"

"No," I replied. "We just recently learned what we were."

She looked past me at Damian, who stood quietly with pleading eyes. Her eyes acknowledged a silent agreement between the two. I narrowed my eyes at him. He knew something more about this prophecy and wasn't telling us. She turned to me and smiled.

"You will learn in due time," she said with a smile.

She climbed atop the fountain and pushed a button. A platform emerged from the water and raised her to the height of the angel so that she could claim the chalice from its hands. The platform retracted, and she stepped down from the fountain. The entire city went dead. No electricity hum, no lights, nothing.

I looked at her, furrowing my brows.

"The manna powered our city. But, when you defeat Alpha, we shall be able to claim the sea top once more as our home," she explained.

"It's just powder. How does it power your city?" I asked.

"It is more than just powder. It is the soul of the universe where the spark first began," she said. "Now, go! You must hurry. The dome will not open without electricity. It has enough of a charge for one more push open, but you must make it there before the energy exhausts itself."

"Thank you," I replied, taking the chalice from her hands.

I pulled the bag out that Starfire had given us to place it in. As soon as the cup touched the inside of the bag, it sealed precisely how she said it would seal around the cup. I tied the cup to my waist and nodded my thanks to the Atlanteans before we turned and ran toward the gate entrance we had come through. I understood what she meant finally. There was a glass fail-safe sliding into place that would lock us in if we didn't get to the outer dome in time. Damian, Xavier, and I pounded down the long bridge, racing the glass seal falling into place. We dropped to our sides, sliding underneath the dome as it locked into place.

"Can we portal from here, or do we have to be seaside?" I asked Damian.

"I'm pretty sure we have to be seaside," he replied. "They must know where to open the portal, and they have never been to Atlantis or know its exact location. They could accidentally suck up the ocean instead."

All the mermaids waited for us at the glass dome, staring at us angrily and hungrily. The Lernaean Hydra still swam around the border of the city as well. I swallowed the lump of fear in my throat as I stared out at the creatures waiting for us to emerge so they could devour us alive.

"Ok, game plan," Damian began. "We open the gate and swim as fast as we can go to the topside."

"Then what? We have no idea where we are in the ocean. Then we swim the rest of the way to the shore?" I asked.

"Well, do you want to return the way we came?" he asked.

"Not really," I replied, exasperated.

"Everyone ready?" Xavier asked, grabbing our hands.

"As ready as can be," I muttered.

We pushed against the dome and were sucked out by the waters and push of air from behind us. I tried holding onto their hands as we somersaulted and spun through the water, but at some point, I let go and was lost in a spiral of water. The mermaids swarmed in on me, grabbing at my body as I struggled against them to free my swords. I clicked the buttons to activate them, and they flashed brightly as if activated by the presence of Seelies. The mermaids backed away slowly from me, seeing the glint of silver. They scowled at me as they parted slowly, creating a path for me to make it back to where Damian and Xavier rested with their swords drawn as well. It was then that the Leviathan swam in, grabbing as many mermaids in its mouth as it could fit. The Lernaean Hydra howled in a rage, almost as if the mermaids belonged to it. A fight ensued between the two gargantuan creatures as we swam as fast as we could the way we had come to Atlantis initially. Everything sped past us in a blur as we held hands and used our powers to propel us through the waters. We made it to the reef in record time and continued until we met a wall and swam upward. We popped from the water, snatching the red caps from our heads so we could breathe the fresh seaside air.

"Hurry, blow on the shell," Damian demanded, looking around on guard for something, anything, to attack us.

I patted myself, realizing I was not the one that had the shell. "Xavier, do you have it?" I asked.

He fished around in his pockets and produced the shell. He put it to his lips, and we all expected a loud trumpet-type sound, but nothing came.

"Did you do it, right?" Damian asked, turning in circles.

"Well, it didn't exactly come with instructions, Damian. She said to just blow into the seashell when we were ready to return," Xavier replied, irritated.

"Do it again!" Damian demanded.

Xavier put the shell to his lips again, huffed in a lungful of air, and blew as hard as he could at the end of the conch. Still, nothing happened.

"I don't like this," I remarked. "What if Alpha got to Starfire?"

"There is no way Alpha could have gotten into Lightshade," Damian replied. "Hair brain over there just isn't doing it right."

Xavier tossed the conch to Damian, who fumbled with it and nearly dropped it. "Well, then you do it, genius."

Damian did the same maneuvers that Xavier had tried, and still, nothing happened. I had an idea after Damian turned red in the face for a third time trying to summon the portal. I lifted my hands that still had the blades snugly fit to them. I waved my hands like Reikal did and pulled my power from within and up to my hands. The knives began to spark bright purple and yellow flames. In front of us appeared a portal remarkably similar to the one Reikal had summoned up, but a bit different. It glowed the same color as the sparks had been, but it wasn't translucent. However, we could see to the other side and saw Starfire, Reikal, and Gwendolyn all sitting around a table talking.

"How did you do that?" Xavier asked.

"Well, if my father could do it, then why can't we?" I asked with a smile.

We stepped through the portal, and it disappeared behind us as those who sat around the table stopped their conversation and looked over at us.

"About time you got back," Starfire said. "We were about to send a search party for your bodies."

"We tried to use the seashell, but it didn't work," Damian replied, handing it back to her.

She laughed. "That was a ruse. I apologize for my joke. I wanted you to use your powers to get back, which I see you finally caught on." She motioned to the bag wrapped around the chalice on my hip. "Is that it?" she asked.

"Yes," I replied, handing the satchel over to her. "We almost weren't allowed to take it. And whatever we needed it for needs to hurry before the people of Atlantis die from not having it."

Starfire nodded, opened the satchel, and carefully pulled the chalice out of the bag. "Excellent," she whispered. "Now, I must get to work on making you the elixir to drink to strip the Seelie enchantment from you."

Starfire stood from the table and ducked into a room to the right, closing the door behind her. Gwendolyn and Reikal sat silently at the table, staring at us.

"You three look… well," Gwendolyn remarked.

"I'm sure we do," I replied, shaking my head. "Where is Praeziel?"

"He left earlier. He went to round up the Nephilim that are willing to fight for the cause," she replied quietly.

"I'm sorry I didn't tell you about your home," Damian spoke softly. "I had no idea you didn't know about what had happened in the Otherworld."

She smiled with appreciation. "It's ok, but thank you."

"Well, I am going to go change out of these wet clothes," I said, breaking the small silence.

Xavier and Damian glanced down at their soaking wet clothes as well, noticing they were leaving puddles on the floor.

"We better go change as well," Xavier remarked, glancing at Damian.

"See you back in a bit," Gwendolyn replied and continued whatever conversation she had been having with Reikal prior to our arrival.

The three of us all headed up to our rooms, ducking in and closing the doors behind us. I pulled the wet pants down and kicked them off into a corner and slipped a warm, dry pair on to replace them. As I was pulling the shirt over my head, I got stuck inside of it. Of course, the shirt would trap me inside of it. It was practically glued to my body already. Once I was able to get it up and over my head, I tossed it over to the wet pants and then slipped a dry shirt on. I slipped my feet back into the comfortable boots I had been wearing and opened my door, heading back downstairs.

I was the first to arrive back at the table. You would think boys wouldn't take as long to change their clothes. It was a possibility that they were exhausted and lay down to sleep. I mingled with Gwendolyn and Reikal at the table and joined in with the chatter they had going, releasing the built-up tension from the day's events from my shoulders as I sipped warm chamomile tea.

Starfire emerged from the room that she had been in with five bottles in her hand.

"It's ready," she said, setting them on the table.

CHAPTER 5

"WHY ARE THERE FIVE?" I asked, staring at the bottles.

"Three are for you three. The other two are for your parents," she replied. "They need their enchantments taken away as well. As soon as they find me, they will be given their elixirs as well."

"How do you know they will find you?" I asked.

"Because I know everything, dear," she replied with a small tug of a smile to her mouth. "I am the Oracle, the all-seeing and all-knowing."

The boys emerged from upstairs no sooner than Starfire had explained everything. Both of their moods were different than what they had been before they went to change. Xavier looked... crushed. That was the only way I could describe his face. I looked at Damian, and his face had the same grim expression.

"You two, ok?" I asked.

"Yes," Damian replied, changing the expression on his face to a light-hearted one.

I glanced at Xavier, and he gave a half-hearted smile in return as well. I knew something was wrong, though, and if I had to beat it out of the two of them, I would eventually find out what it was. Starfire pushed the three vials of the elixir to the center of the table.

"Drink up," she said with a smile.

I picked up a vial and uncorked the bottle. I thought it would smell horrible, but it actually smelled sweet and flowery. Damian uncorked his as well, giving it a sniff. Xavier just stared at his cup, almost as if he didn't want to drink it.

"You too," Starfire said, pointing at Xavier. "You need to drink it as well, or it won't work for you three at all." There was a look in her eye, almost as if she knew something that Xavier knew, but no one else did.

Xavier picked his vial up and uncorked it like Damian and I had done. He gave it a sniff, and his face seemed pleased at the smell of it.

"Bottoms up," I said, and we all turned the vials up at the same time and downed the contents.

The elixir was just as sweet as it smelled but had a bitter aftertaste to it. I set the vial down on the table and waited for something to happen. I looked over at Damian and Xavier to see if there were any noticeable changes with them as well. They were checking themselves over just as I had. I looked at Starfire, who watched us carefully as we reacted to the potion.

"Nothing is happening," I replied with a shrug, setting the bottle down on the table.

No sooner had the words left my lips than pain tore through my stomach. I doubled over, almost as if I would vomit the contents back up. I wretched and took deep breaths as the pain radiated throughout my body. I heard Damian and Xavier react the same way I did.

"You poisoned us?" I asked in disbelief.

"No, my child. No one said this transformation was going to be easy," she replied, stroking my hair. "It gets worse before it gets better."

I fell to the ground, writhing in searing pain. It felt as if I were back in the Lake of Fire again, and the gasoline was fueling the fire within my veins. I screamed out in pain as the fire burned from my stomach and throughout my entire body. I heard Damian and Xavier's screams alongside mine. Steam rose from my skin, and fire crackled to the top. The more I burned outwardly, the worse it felt inwardly. But no matter how my skin blazed, nothing else in the room caught fire. Almost at the moment I was giving up and submitting to the imminent death from the toxic potion roiling through my veins, the pain began to subside. The nerve endings that had popped and frayed, burning to a crisp, came back to life, and I could feel the coolness of the air sweep over me. I sat up, with sweat dripping from my body and breathing deeply. I still didn't feel any different than I had prior to drinking the ancient substance.

I stood from the floor and dusted off my clothes. I watched as Damian and Xavier did the same, and we all looked at Starfire.

"You are almost ready," she stated. "But before you can move forward, there is one more thing you have to do."

"What's that?" I asked.

She looked at Damian and Xavier, who exchanged glances. "You have to fulfill the prophecy," she replied. "Damian and Xavier already know what the prophecy states."

She placed a book in the middle of the table and flipped it open to a page. My Enochian was a bit rusty, but the header on the page read "Shining Ones." I looked up at Damian and Xavier.

"You both have read this?" I asked.

Damian shook his head. "I have read it. Xavier has not, but he knows the basics of what it says," he replied quietly.

I quietly read through the pages of the ancient language when I reached the part about the prophecy. I slammed the book shut and threw it across the room.

"No!" I yelled. "It lies!"

"It is not a lie, child," Starfire replied. "It is inevitable."

"I won't do it," I replied angrily, looking at Xavier. "There has to be another way."

"There is no other way," Damian said. "You saw the vision in your nightmare just as well as I did. If we don't do it, we lose to Alpha."

"I'm not doing it!" I seethed. "End of discussion!"

I stomped from the room and ran up the stairs to my room, slamming the door behind me. I leaned against the door and sank to the floor below. The words of the prophecy haunted my vision as I squeezed my eyes shut. I buried my face in my legs and cried. This can't be the only way! This is not going to happen! I won't let it!

A soft knock came to the door.

"Go away," I yelled.

"Can I come in, Luxina, please?" Xavier asked on the other side of the door.

I stood from my seated position and turned around, opening the door. He stood there with an unimaginable look of pain on his face. I motioned for him to enter the room. He walked over to the bed and sat down.

"We will find another way," I spouted off before he could speak. "This is not going to happen."

He patted the bed beside him. I sat down and leaned my head against his shoulder. He wrapped his arms around me, placing his chin on my forehead.

"It's not that bad," he replied.

"How can you say that?" I asked. "You will die!"

"I won't die," he replied, gently rocking me in his arms. "I will just become part of you. I am you. I always felt different, almost as if I shouldn't exist. I always thought it was because of my loneliness. It wasn't that. This whole time, it was because I really never was supposed to exist."

"Don't say that," I cried into his shirt. "Your life has meaning! You mean so much to me!"

"And you mean a lot to me," he replied. "That is why I am not upset by this. I will always be a part of you. I will always be there."

"But why? Why did this happen?" I asked. "Why would the universe cause this to happen?"

"It was an accident. When the power of the heavenly portal diminished, and the power between our mother and father was split, our power split as well," he replied.

We stayed that way for a while. Both of us silently cried into one another. I had to absorb Xavier and therein, reabsorb the part of myself that had always been missing. The darkness that my father had to experience that I had never felt. It wasn't like someone had just sucked the darkness away from me. It was sentient. It was a person. And I loved that person dearly.

"Do we have to do it now?" I asked.

"I'm not sure," he replied. "All I know is it has to be done before the final battle with Alpha."

"I want to keep you as long as I can…"

"Soon, you will have me forever," he replied. "And there is no greater gift that I would give than to give you the chance to live."

I buried my face into his chest, and he squeezed me tightly.

"I love you, Xavier," I whispered. "Forever and always."

"You're supposed to," he replied. "You had to learn to love yourself. Our father, when he was created, didn't understand how to love the darkness. He didn't know how to love himself. You were given a gift by seeing the dark of you and being able to love it. You were given the gift of self-love, Luxina. It may hurt in the end, knowing that all what you felt, the power, the love, the moments, was nothing more than moments with yourself and not your other half. But remember the memories. There will always be memories."

We stood from the bed and made our way back downstairs. Starfire had already retired for the evening, so it was just Damian and Gwendolyn sitting at the table, talking quietly. Reikal had already left to go home. Damian's eyes caught mine as I walked into the room, and he quickly looked away.

"You knew this whole time and didn't tell us," I sneered.

He looked down, ashamed. "I was going to do it at the right moment. The last few days happened in a blur. I just couldn't find the right time to tell you."

"The Atlantean leader, she knew, and you asked her not to say anything, didn't you?" I asked heatedly.

"Yes, I didn't want you finding out from a complete stranger in the middle of an important mission," he replied. "I'm sorry."

"I bet you are," I jeered. "That's why you have been buttering up to me so much. Because you read what the prophecy said in full."

"I was not buttering up to you," he replied angrily. "Every emotion I have shown you and experienced has been real and not a ruse. Excuse me for trying to take the time to show you that I wasn't a bad person."

He stood from the table and walked to the door.

"Where are you going? Running away?" I asked nastily.

"You're not my mother, Luxina. Stop acting like her. That's how you get pushed away," he said, walking out the door.

"Well, maybe it would be better if you pushed me away. I trusted you. And you couldn't even share this secret you knew with me. It seems like everyone knew but Xavier and me. How fair is that?"

He stopped short in the door frame. "I'm sorry," he said once more and then left the cottage.

I followed him. "No, you don't get to walk away from this!"

"Luxina, leave me be," he replied through gritted teeth, balling his hands into fists.

"Oh, you're getting angry. Join the club," I shouted.

The heat began to rise through my body, and I got angrier. I didn't want it to stop. I wanted to lash out at everything I could. I wanted to burn everything to the ground. Damian whipped around, his eyes glowing brighter than I had ever seen them glow before.

"You want to blame someone? Blame Starfire. She was the one that dropped the book for me to read before I had to escape a pit of death Alpha had arranged for me. Do you really think that was the one thing that was at the forefront of my mind? I ran for DAYS from creatures you could never dream of. Oh, wait, you did! Those creatures in your nightmare, I fought. Alone. I nearly died. From the moment I have been with you all, I have been staving off attack after attack from countless creatures trying to kill us all. So, excuse me, princess, that I didn't call a timeout to all those things to fill you in on details I had just told Xavier about prior to Starfire handing you that damned forsaken book."

He walked up to me as I searched for the words to reply to him. He grabbed my hands in his, and I looked deep into his bright eyes.

"I did this all for you," he stammered. "Why can't you see my worth? Why must I be blamed for everything that goes wrong?"

He let my hands go and placed his hands gently around my face.

"I don't care what happens to me as long as you are safe. I gave up my life to keep you and Xavier safe. I laid down my sword and admitted defeat in that ring before your dad yanked me from it. If I was dead, you would be safe. Alpha could no longer use you two against me, and I wasn't a threat to your safety." His eyes searched my eyes, pleading with me to believe what he was saying. "But I will never be more than Alpha's little monster to you."

He let my face go and ran in the opposite direction, disappearing into the thick brush. I just stood there, stunned. Is that what he really thought? Was that how I treated him? Keeping him at arm's length and only letting him in when I was vulnerable. Did I really still think of him as Alpha's little monster? No, of course, I didn't. I thought of each time he was at my side, pulling me to safety, sacrificing his own life to ensure that I was protected. It was then that I realized how everything was true. It was why Xavier kept to himself and away from me. I didn't want to save myself. So, Xavier's personality and mood changed. Is that how it worked?

I sat on the ground and pulled my knees to my chest. I waited. I waited for Damian to return. I waited so I could apologize for everything. I needed to tell him. I needed to show him that he wasn't a monster to me. I needed him to know I honestly did care about him. I waited for hours. The sun beat down on me, but I didn't move from the spot I sat. However, no matter how long I sat waiting, he did not reappear. I buried my face in my knees. I screw up everything.

"You do not screw up everything," Xavier said, sitting down on the ground next to me. "You just pushed his buttons is all. He will be back. You will apologize, and he will forgive you."

"No, he won't," I croaked. "I'm too broken to love. I'm too broken to understand. I'm broken beyond repair. This whole mess of things is my fault. There were so many things I could have done differently."

Xavier wrapped his arm around me and pulled me into his chest. "You are not broken beyond repair."

"That doesn't help when it comes from you," I replied, burying my face into his arm.

"He is hurting over this as much as you are," he said, rocking me. "He has to lose a brother."

I hadn't even thought of that. I felt even more horrible for the way I acted, as if I was the only one who mattered.

"Are you sure he will forgive me?" I asked, peeking up at him from his shirt.

"How could he not? I would," he replied with a light laugh.

"And you're ok with everything else?" I asked.

"It makes more and more sense the more I think about it all," he replied. "I came to terms with it easier than either of you did."

"We could still try and figure out a different way," I protested.

"No," he replied. "I'm ready to go home."

"And where is home for you?" I asked.

"Home is in your soul," he murmured.

"How do you suppose we do it?" I asked, trying to picture my body absorbing him, but the vision came out of me eating him instead.

"That I don't know," he replied. "But I am ready when you are."

He stood from the ground and offered his hand to help me up. As I stood from the ground, Praeziel came down the path from the portal at the top of the mountain. I half expected to see an army of Nephilim following him, but he was alone. I wonder if they declined to help fight in the war against Alpha. Xavier and I met him as he reached the bottom of the path.

"I see you all made it back in one piece," he said with a light smile. "Where is Damian?"

"Cooling off," Xavier replied.

He nodded as if he understood. He looked at me with sympathetic eyes. "I take it Starfire shared the prophecy with you upon your return?" he asked.

I dropped my eyes, nodding. "When did you find out about it?" I asked.

"She told Gwendolyn and me after you all departed on your quest to Atlantis. It was then I thought it would be best to go and gather the Nephilim," he replied.

"Were you successful?" I asked.

"They will be here in the morning," he replied with a nod. "Our numbers against Alpha are growing. We have the Nephilim, what is left of the Watchers, and those that made it to safety in the Otherworld."

"Add that to the numbers of angels there are in the Summit, and we have a decent team," Xavier said.

"Let's pray that is so," Praeziel replied. "Something tells me Alpha has more up his sleeve than what we are aware of."

"You happen to be very correct," Damian said as he emerged from the brush. He refused to look at me. "Alpha has made all kinds of new creations. I had just a taste of them in the arena. If my dream is right, he has millions upon millions of these things made and stashed away."

"Ah, Praeziel," Starfire interrupted, stepping out onto her porch. "Right on time. Fill us all in on your little adventure." She motioned for him to come inside.

Praeziel took the forefront, and we all headed toward the cottage. As they started up the steps, I snagged Damian by the hand and pulled him back to me. Xavier stopped and turned around to see if he was needed.

"We will catch up in just a few," I said, reassuring him we were okay.

Damian stepped down from the step he was on and stood before me. I had never paid attention to most details about him. He had freckles across his creamy white skin. His eyes were a penetrating color of blue, but not just any blue. It looked as if I was staring straight into the galaxy. Different shades and flecks of blue popped here and there the closer you examined them. He was much taller than me, almost by a foot. When you looked at his red curly hair, you could see streaks of white mixed into the different hues of fire that grew. His hair was shorter than the last time I remembered seeing it. His skin had small scars that had long ago healed and were just pale patches of skin slightly raised. His eyelashes were long and white and almost seemed to flutter as he opened and closed his eyes.

He never once faltered with his gaze as I took in every part of his body, memorizing them each for the first time. He stood there quietly as I took my hands and ran them down the sides of his neck, almost but not quite touching his skin where the scars of his torture were visible. I looked up into his soft eyes, pleading with my own, searching through them to see if I would know the answer before I spoke.

"I'm sorry," I whispered.

He looked away quickly, and I turned his face back to mine. I wanted him to see that what he believes about himself is not what I believe. I wanted him to read it from my soul.

"You're not a monster," I gently spoke. "You are not what Alpha tried to make you into."

"You say it, but you don't mean it. I saw the way you looked at me. You will never see me for more than what I have been showcased as," he replied, pushing past me.

"I need you as much as you need me," I stated without turning around to see if he even stopped. "I will forever need you."

"That's the problem. You need me," he replied, walking upright behind me to stand, hesitant to continue. "But you don't want me."

He turned swiftly on his heels and walked inside the cottage, leaving me alone with his words. Every emotion I had been fighting since meeting him came rushing to the top. I didn't need to feel him. I wanted to feel him. I didn't need him by my side. I wanted him by my side. It was then that I realized I had been fighting against so many things regarding him. I was afraid of ending up like my mother and choosing the wrong person. I pitied him when he took me from my father, but I felt compassion for him because I knew that he was being made to do it against his will. This whole time I had been fighting this welling, overwhelming feeling inside for him because I honestly believed that Xavier and I were twin flames like our parents. But now, since that is all said and done and over with, I knew what the flutter in my stomach had meant when Damian touched me gently with his hands.

It was simple to realize once I stopped looking at Xavier as if he were anything more than an extension of myself. Yes, I loved Xavier, but there was just an energetic feeling. But within Xavier was a piece of myself that also reflected Damian. Xavier was everything Damian was, and Damian was so much more than Xavier. I watched them from the door as they spoke and easily got along. The piece I was missing from within that would attach so easily to Damian was in Xavier. If I were ever to really genuinely care for Damian, Xavier had to meld with me. It was pretty unfair. Once a sentient being sparks into existence, even if it was never meant to exist, it is unfair to snuff its light out. But, as I stare at Xavier, I can see it. I can see the glamour the universe had put up. A mirror stood before me, and I saw reflected back a dark-haired me. I saw what darkness would look like on the outside. The confidence I lacked. Everything represented by the shadows of your ego.

Both of them looked up and saw me watching them, arms crossed leaning against the door jam. My eyes rested briefly on Xavier, switching to Damian's face, and my stomach knotted and flip-flopped when I reached his eyes. It felt like heartbreak racing through my heart while simultaneously being elated. I turned and walked away from the door out into the small yard that surrounded Starfire's cottage. I started walking without knowing where my feet were carrying me. My walk turned into a jog that quickly developed into a sprint. I was running without a clue as to where I was going. But it felt like that's what I needed to do. Was I running away from my problems? I most likely was, but the exhilaration of the wind whipping past my face made it feel like I was flying, which is what I wanted to do most of all.

I quickly found myself deep in the thicket of the woods. The smell of dirt and plants filled my nostrils, and I breathed the heady petrichor scent in deeply. I still continued my run. I followed a creek and watched as tiny little creatures with pincers buried in the dirt beneath the running water. The creek bed became broader and deeper, and I was soon following along the banks of a river. Birds soared overhead, and fish jumped and splashed back down in the river. I looked across the river, and a family of deer stood there foraging and drinking water. The river picked up speed, and I raced it, my feet pounding the forest floor as I ran freely without a care in the world.

I heard a thunderous roar as the river ended and flowed over the side of a cliff, forming a waterfall. As I grew closer and closer to the edge of the cliff, preparing to jump and dive into the water, I closed my eyes and held my arms out. I was tackled to the ground from the side and rolled with my assailant until we came to a stop in a blanket of moss. I opened my eyes, and Damian rested on top of my body.

"What did you do that for?" I asked, breathless from the running.

"Do you have a death wish?" he asked angrily. "You didn't even look to see what was on the other side of the cliff before you tried to jump."

"I would have been fine!" I retorted. "Why were you following me, anyway?" I asked heatedly.

"To make sure you didn't do something dumb or death-defying," he shot back.

"Why do you care?!" I shouted.

"Because you are all I have," he replied, pounding the ground beside me. "You're all I will have left."

I ran my hands through his hair and pulled his face to mine. "Do you love me?" I asked. "Not like you would love Xavier. Do you love me? Do you want me, or do you need me?"

"I could ask you the same things," he replied.

My heart raced in my chest. My fingers brushed his lips and danced across his face. I knew my answer. I had been fighting it for too long. The fight was now over.

"I-"

Damian jumped from the spot he had been in, hovering over my body. "No," he said firmly. He paced back and forth in front of me. "No," he said again, shaking his head and pounding his fists against his ears.

"Damian, are you ok?" I asked, rising from the ground.

He covered his ears and howled in pain. His screams tore through the empty forest, echoing and bouncing back. I went to grab him, to try and help him, but he grabbed my hands and pushed them away.

"Go!" he demanded. "Go… now!" he squeezed out distraughtly.

"What is it? What's wrong?" I asked in a craze.

I tried to touch him, and he just pushed me off and put his hands back over his ears.

"Just go, Luxina!" he demanded again.

I remembered the promise I had made him after the werewolf attack. *When I tell you to go, just do as I ask.*

"I'll go get help," I stammered. "I'll be back for you!"

"No, don't!" he cried. "It's Alpha... I don't know... I might hurt someone!" he screamed.

"You won't hurt me!" I yelled, grabbing his face to stare into his eyes. "You're not what Alpha made you. You can fight this!"

He pushed me down to the ground and was on top of me. As his fist came down, I rolled out of the way as it met the ground below. I barrel-rolled into a crouched position and waited for him to make another move. I saw him fight whatever force he was grappling with in his head. His fists pounded the sides of his ears, and he doubled over, shaking his head to rid himself of whatever was fighting internally in his brain. Whatever he heard, I could not. I don't know if it was some kind of low pitch frequency he was picking up or if Alpha was talking directly into his brain. But when he turned to stare at me, his eyes had blacked over. He glared and ran at me. He started throwing jabs that I parried and kicked away. My hands moved with precision as his assault came faster and stronger. I did a backflip and kicked out at the same time, striking him in the chest and pushing him back. I landed in a crouch and swooped my leg around.

He jumped over it, coming down with another punch. I grabbed his arm, twisted it, and then flipped him over my shoulder. He landed with a thud, swiping me from my feet with his leg. I tucked and rolled as I landed, and his foot barely grazed me as he hammered it to the ground.

We were back on our feet, jabbing and parrying every attempted move by the other. He grabbed his ears again, screaming in pain.

"Leave!" he screeched.

"No, not this time," I replied.

I did a roundabout kick, catching him in the temple, and he went down. He didn't move, and I panicked for a moment, thinking I may have killed him. I ran to him and checked his breathing. I watched as his chest rose and fell and breathed a sigh of relief. Now what? I had to get him back to the cottage and tie him up before he woke back up. There was no way I could lift him and carry him all the way back. I had run a few miles deep into the woods. I looked into my hands and thought of giving another portal a shot. I didn't have the knives Reikal had given me this time, so I hoped it would work.

I reached deep within me and pulled with everything in me, waving my hands as a whirlwind appeared before me. I could see everyone sitting around the table. I grabbed Damian underneath his armpits and pulled him with all my might into the room before dismissing the portal. Everyone jumped from the table and rushed to his side.

"What happened?" Xavier asked. "Were you two attacked?" He looked at the scratches all over my body.

"No," I replied. "We need to tie him up. Alpha hijacked him."

"What do you mean Alpha hijacked him?" Praeziel asked.

"We were talking, and then all a sudden, he started talking to himself, screaming no. He grabbed his ears and told me to leave. I stayed to offer him help. That was when his eyes went black like the demons' eyes, and he attacked me," I explained.

"He was probably a spy this whole time, waiting to get the elixir from Starfire so he could become Alpha's weapon," Gwendolyn remarked.

Fire tore through my body. "That is NOT the case at all! He is not a monster! He is not Alpha's toy! He is suffering! He is innocent!"

Everyone took a step back from me as my skin began to sizzle.

"This is what Alpha wants you to believe. He wants you to think Damian is playing sides so that we will send his weapon back to him. It's not going to happen. Now, grab some rope and tie him up in a chair!" I demanded.

"The only thing that can stop his powers is something that is made with unicorn hair," Xavier replied quietly.

"I have just the thing," Starfire replied, hurrying into a room adjacent to the one we stood. She returned just as quickly, carrying some chains. "These were given to me in case of fail-safe measures." She dropped them on the table.

Everyone just stared at the chains and then at Damian. They didn't like this idea one bit. I didn't like it either, but I sure as hell wasn't handing him back over to Alpha now. And anyone that tried to stop me from protecting him would quickly become my enemy. I grabbed the chains from the table. Xavier and Praeziel hoisted Damian up into a chair. They tied his legs to the chair legs, wrapped the rope around his upper body, and then I placed the manacles around his wrists behind his back.

I pulled a chair up to face him and waited for him to regain consciousness.

"You all can leave if you wish," I stated curtly. "I have this handled."

Praeziel and Gwendolyn left the room. Xavier stayed behind with me as Damian's eyelids fluttered to life. I hoped I would see the blue of his eyes staring at me, but all that was there were the cavernous eyes of an abyss. He glared and tried to free himself of his ties. Once it proved futile, he leaned back in the chair and relaxed with a malicious grin spreading from ear to ear.

"You think you can stop me, but you can't," he stated coolly. "I will be triumphant in the end."

"I want to speak to Damian," I replied calmly.

"You're speaking to Damian," Damian replied. "Although, you may not recognize him with all this power staring at you."

"I want to speak to Damian," I once again stated calmly.

"Damian isn't here!" he hissed. "How are you fairing, Luxina? You don't look well."

I glared at him. It was Alpha.

"Oh, you just realized who is speaking through Damian. This is too fabulous. Now tell me, dear, what was it like when you found out that all along, I had been keeping your real twin flame hostage? Were you angry? Were you sad?" He paused for a minute, and a smile spread across his face. "Oh, you didn't think I knew about the prophecy. Why do you think I was so adamant about getting you and Xavier back here, or should I say you and your split personality?" He turned his head toward Xavier. "Tell me, boy, how does it feel to know that you were never meant to exist and, honestly, really don't exist at this moment? How does it feel knowing you have to give up your life to save the universe?" Xavier stood emotionless, staring at Alpha. "Oh, that's right. Whatever she feels is how you feel." He looked back at me. "Am I right so far?"

I didn't acknowledge a single word he was saying to us. I stared blankly at him with the poker face that Damian uses so well to hide things.

"So, tell me, where exactly are you? Are you really safe? Or are the ones you are with secretly plotting against you?" he asked with a crooked grin. "Can you trust your traveling group? Are they really on your side? Or are they with me?" He laughed heartily. "Oh, how wonderful would it be for you to genuinely believe that the Seelies have pledged their devotion to you. Tell me, how is young Gwendolyn doing? Still catching rabbits for you to eat? Did you ever wonder why it was she that led you through all the portals through the Otherworld, and you could never quite catch Starfire that had never moved once?"

There must have been a flicker in my eyes because his grin spread from ear to ear.

"That's right, Luxina. Starfire has been in the same exact spot for many years. I just can't get through her firewall."

I glanced nervously at Xavier as he chewed on a nail.

"I want Damian back," I stated once more calmly. "I want him back now."

"You're going to have to battle me for him. I have control of his mind right now. Would you like to fight for him? Meet me in the meadow. I won't really be there, of course, but you're going to have to be strong enough to pull him back to the surface." He glanced at Xavier. "Sacrifice one to save the other…"

He smiled evilly at me, and I couldn't help but glare back.

"Starfire!" I called out.

She appeared from her room, awaiting my request.

"Find something to put him to sleep," I said. "Something that will knock him out for a while."

She nodded and disappeared off into the alchemy room. She returned with a potion bottle. Damian smiled and took the potion without a fuss. He immediately slumped unconscious in his chair.

"Ok, one problem down," I said.

"What's the next one?" Xavier asked.

"You know the answer to that," I replied, standing from my chair and looking upstairs. Gwendolyn stood at the rail of the balcony where our rooms were. I wasn't sure how long she had been standing there, listening to the conversation. Her face didn't show any signs of her being caught in the deceptive lies she had been telling us for the past year.

"Starfire?" I asked quietly, not taking my eyes off Gwendolyn.

"Yes, child?" she replied.

"I just need to know one thing," I stated calmly.

"What do you need to know, child?" she replied.

"Have you been here our entire journey, or have you been bouncing from place to place?" I asked.

"I have lived here my entire life," she replied quietly.

"Thank you," I replied without drawing attention to what my hands were doing. "That was all I needed to know." I clicked my knife's button to activate it as soon as I tossed it through the air. It came to life in the middle of the air and landed squarely in the middle of Gwendolyn's chest. It was one of the knives that Damian had specially crafted for him by the Dark Queen Mab. Gwendolyn slammed into the wall behind her from the force of the blow and slowly sat down on the floor. She couldn't even pull the knife from her chest as the handle was made from iron as well.

"Praeziel," she croaked.

Praeziel emerged from his room and, upon notice of her condition, ran to her side.

"Stop, Praeziel," I commanded.

Xavier had already pulled out his bow and arrows and had them pointed at Praeziel. Praeziel put his hands slowly in the air and backed away from Gwendolyn.

"Did you know?" I asked.

"Did I know what?" he asked heatedly.

"That Gwendolyn was working for Alpha?" I questioned.

"She was not working for Alpha," he seethed. "She would never betray me!"

"Ask Starfire where she has lived this entire time, then," I replied. "Ask her if every time we thought we were close to her, she moved. The birds, the trees, nature, telling Gwendolyn when she went alone into the woods that Starfire had uprooted again. Ask Starfire where she has lived this past year."

He looked at Starfire, the answer already ringing true in his mind. Gwendolyn had lied to us all. He looked at her as she wept, the blood seeping down the front of her chest from the blade buried deep within her cavity.

"Why?" he cried, hitting his knees.

"I don't know," she replied quietly.

Blood began to trickle down from the corners of her mouth. Praeziel stood from her side and drew his sword from its sheath.

"I'm sorry," she whispered.

Without hesitation, he cut her head clean from her body. He pulled my knife from her body and tossed it to the floor where I stood.

"I suggest you do it as well," he stated somberly. "If I can do it, you can too. Drive a knife through his heart before this world goes to hell."

He walked back into his room and shut the door behind him. I returned my gaze to Damian, soundly asleep in the chair in front of me. His head had lolled to where it now hung to his chest.

"He isn't right, but he isn't wrong either," Starfire said. "You either must break Damian free forever from the clutches of Alpha, or you will have to watch the world die. There is no middle ground."

"I don't even know how to save him," I replied.

"There is only one way to save him now," she replied, looking at Xavier.

I closed my eyes and breathed in deeply. I wasn't ready for this. There were people he still needed to say goodbye to. Alpha had played the chess game, and I was at the final move. I could either bring my queen out and put her in position to take his king, or I could move my knight, and he takes my king. Sacrifice one to save the other...

"Hey," Xavier said, breaking my deep thoughts. "I already told you. I am ready when you are. I'm just going home."

I nodded. I knew what we had to do. We had to meet in the meadow like we always used to. That is where my ego and shadow self lived. My psyche was whole there.

"Starfire, can you help us slip into sleep?" I asked, tears glistening down my face.

She nodded and left the room. Xavier reached over and squeezed my hand.

"Let's go save the world," he said with a smile.

CHAPTER 6

XAVIER AND I LAY side by side in my bed, our hands intertwined as we waited for the sleep potion that Starfire had given us to kick in. This one wasn't as strong as the sedative she had given to Damian, so we had to drift off to sleep naturally. I moved and draped my arm across his chest. He squeezed me tighter in response. My eyelids began to grow heavy and droop in exhaustion. It had been days since I had fallen asleep. The inky, dark background of my mind washed over me, and I felt myself tumbling down a black hole.

I sat up in the middle of our field. Xavier and Damian were nowhere to be seen. Where were they? I stood from the ground and dusted my clothes off. The grass had grown back from the devastation Alpha had wreaked upon the valley. Our tree stood behind me, green and vibrant with leaves and flowers. The wheatgrass gently blew in the breeze as bees buzzed and birds chirped.

I felt a tap on my shoulder and turned to find Damian standing behind me.

"Beautiful, isn't it?" he asked.

His eyes were still deep pools of black. I looked frantically around for Xavier, but he had not shown up yet.

"Waiting for your other half, I presume," Damian remarked. "Are you sure he will come?" he asked.

"Yes," I replied firmly.

"You put your faith in so many people," he laughed. "I mean, you trusted Gwendolyn. Look at where that got you."

"You're the reason Gwendolyn betrayed us," I retorted.

"Me? Who do you believe you are speaking to right now?" he mused.

"I know it's Alpha talking through you," I replied. "You have to fight him, Damian!"

"No, Luxina," he replied. "This is all me. This is who I truly am."

"No, it isn't," I hissed. "You are not what he made you. You are more than that."

"How do you know? How do you know that I am not evil?" he demanded. "How do you know I won't kill you right here, right now? You don't!"

"Yes, I do know the answer to that," I replied heatedly. "You told me yourself I am the only person that could ever kill you because you would never hurt me."

"That was the weak me," he snickered, grinning. "The strong me thinks otherwise."

I grabbed his face and stared into his eyes. "Come back to me, Damian."

He leaned in close and whispered, "I am right here."

"Leave her alone," Xavier said, walking to where we stood.

"Oh, the faithful lapdog shows his face," Damian sneered. "Ready to dissolve away into nothing?" he asked. "Because that's all you are. You are nothing. Nonexistent."

Xavier's face didn't waver a moment with Damian's words. "There is nothing you can say to me to hurt me."

"No, but I can kill you, can't I?" Damian asked.

"You won't hurt me," Xavier replied. "You won't hurt either of us. You had plenty of chances to do so before. The real Damian, not the one Alpha tries to control. He would never hurt us."

"That you know of," Damian replied. "Tell me, how much do you know about me? Do you really know the pain and torment I faced at the hand of Alpha? Can you feel it? Can you feel every stroke of the whip that burned into my body? No, you can't. You have absolutely no idea what it is to feel what I feel or to know what I know."

"I can," I replied. "I can feel it. I can see it. I know your anguish and your despair, and you are nothing like the person you think you are. You don't even know what you are. You think the world doesn't know, but I do. No one will ever know you as I do!"

I grabbed his shirt and pulled him close to me. I placed my hand on his forehead, and with everything in me, I willed every moment we had ever shared together into his mind. What he felt, what I felt, what happened, the experiences, they all rushed through his mind until he passed out, hitting the ground.

"We don't have much time," I croaked in tears to Xavier.

Xavier and I walked to the tree and stood embraced in front of it. The tree that sparked so many memories between us now would be an empty reminder of the moments I had spent here with Xavier. Never again would I see his face or hear his laugh. I wouldn't be able to reach out to him in the middle of the night for comfort. I would never be able to experience him as a person ever again.

The petals on the tree began to fall and float in the breeze as we stood and embraced in front of it. It looked like our walk through the Otherworld as the Forget-Me-Trees shed their petals all around us. He squeezed me tighter.

"I should have been kinder to you than I was," he said to me as he kissed my forehead.

"I wanted to be pushed away. That is why you did it. It's not your fault," I replied.

"There are so many things I want to tell you," he whispered.

"I'm sure I will find out," I replied in quiet breaths.

He placed his forehead against mine, and our bodies began to burn lightly. I stared into his eyes, and he matched my stare. His eyes began to glow that bright light I had always admired.

"Yours do, too," he said, and I knew what he meant without asking.

His body began to glow brighter, and I could see the same light swirl around me as well. We placed our hands together, palms out, and the energy crash crackled through the air. His skin felt like fire the brighter he burned. I felt myself grow weightless as our bodies began to float lightly above the ground. Lights like the light that shot from all three of us now swirled in tiny orbs around us. His body was nothing but one bright light.

"Never forget me," he whispered.

"I could never forget you," I whispered back. "But what if I can't feel you? I am not worthy of this."

"I am the dark of you," he replied softly. "I will always be there. You just must listen. Listen to my call. I will be there with you through it all."

The entire valley was lit with a blinding white light, forcing me to shut my eyes, and I felt a tearing pain in my body. Everything went dark around me, and I slowly opened my eyes as the burning feeling slowly faded away. Xavier was gone. I stood alone in the middle of the field. Empty but whole. The missing part that I had never known was missing now rested in my soul. Tears spilled from my eyes, and I hit the ground on my knees. Fire sprang to my skin and traveled to the tree we shared. Slowly, inch by inch, the tree caught fire. The petals that had blown so beautifully from the tree before were now ashen petals of regret and shame that floated softly to the ground. Light fires began to sprout in the field as the dry wheat grass caught aflame from the glowing embers. I screamed out in rage and pain. I screamed out in fear and doubt. I screamed out in hatred and self-loathing.

I balled my flaming hands together, pressing them to my chest in anguish. If I couldn't save Damian, I really was forever alone now. It didn't matter if I was whole. I couldn't feel anything that was supposed to signal the completion of my soul. I didn't feel Xavier's presence. I felt nothing but a numb, drowning, sinking feeling welling within my heart. I looked off into the field to see if Damian had woken up yet. He stood in the center of the wildfire blazing out of control in the field, watching me silently. It felt like time stood still or was going by in slow motion. He slowly began to walk toward me, and the fires in the field froze over in his wake. Fire and ice— what a pair. He stopped before me, his eyes still black as death. He would kill me now, but honestly, I didn't even care any longer.

He dropped to his knees in front of me and stared into my swollen eyes. He didn't say a word. He just sat there quietly. The finality of everything was finally sinking in. A tear slid down his face and turned to ice as it dropped to the ground.

"He's gone?" he breathed.

My face contorted, and I nodded yes, tears falling freely down my face while swallowing the lump in my throat. The tears came one by one down his face. He leaned his head against my forehead.

"No, no, not yet," he whispered over and over.

"He did it for you," I replied, choking on the words. "I did it for you."

Silence fell between us as we sat there, forehead to forehead.

"I can't feel him," I cried, my lips quivering. "He's not there. I can't hear him or feel him like we thought."

"I can feel him," he replied, choking on his tears. "I can't," he started gulping air. "I can't be here."

"No!" I cried out, grabbing his face. "Please, please don't leave me too. Don't let me go. There's nothing left but you. Don't leave me! Stay with me, Damian!" I called out to him with everything in me. "Stay with me," I whispered, my heart pounding in my chest.

He stared into my eyes and reached his hand out to my face. He stroked my face ever so softly and gently. His other hand followed suit, and he was holding my face in his hands, gazing into my eyes so intently. "Always."

He leaned in, pulling my face close into his, and pressed his lips against mine. The light exploded between us. A light that was so different from whatever had happened with Xavier and me. Colors swirled around us: pinks, blues, purples.

The colors of the galaxy. I knew now what it looked like. I had every memory Xavier had ever experienced tucked away in my mind. He was here. He was me. The dark of me shining the light in the dark like tiny little stars in the sky. A thought that had never occurred to me prior to that. Darkness isn't just about an inky blackness that engulfs you. It holds the key to whatever light is hiding within you, waiting to explode out. It comes first, in waves, and just when you think that is all there is, the light leaps forward as if it were being sheltered by the dark the entire time. It was almost as if the darkness was protecting the light from any harm that it would incur. Darkness doesn't hold you back. Darkness helps you learn to spread your wings and take off into the light like a baby bird.

Our kiss deepened, and his arms wrapped around me tighter and tighter. I was lost in the moment. Everything that I had held back exploded from within me. Ashes rained down all around us, and bits of snow fell from the sky. Our bodies smoldered against one another as they momentarily became one. My hands roamed freely through his curly locks of hair, bringing his face urgently down over and over as his lips met mine fervently.

"I love you," I whispered in his ear, laying my head on his shoulder.

"I have waited so long to hear those words," he murmured. "I didn't even know I wanted you until I knew I was destined to be with you. And the moment it became clear how our future was going to go, I wanted to protect you. I wanted to love you. I wanted to be the one that held you, calmed your fears, and wiped away your tears."

I opened my closed eyes and looked into his. Those piercing blue eyes were back, with a subtle gray hue to them. His red locks had been replaced as well with solid white hair. I looked at my hair strands that fell around my shoulders, and they were the same color. I guess this was one of the traits of what we really were. He took my hand and led me to the center of the field, and we laid down in the middle of it, wrapped in one another's arms. We watched, mesmerized, as the snow, fire, and ash fell down around us. I reached out with my hand to catch a snowflake and saw the blaze of fire glowing on my hand. He touched my hand with his, which was equally glowing with an icy fire.

His fingers intertwined with mine, and he brought our hands down to his bare chest. My fingers roamed the places he wouldn't allow me to touch before. I touched every single scar that was left from Alpha's hand, ever so gently.

"I could stay here forever with you," he murmured, running his hand through my now white hair. "Don't ever let me go?" he asked.

"Close your eyes," I whispered as I ran my hand over his face, his eyes fluttering closed as I touched his skin. "This is what forever will always feel like because I won't."

He opened his eyes to look at me. My face rushed with heat as his fingers traced my mouth. I started to look away, to look at the field, when he gently pulled my face back to his.

"Don't," he said. "Everything is on fire."

"Come morning," I began, "we will be safe and sound."

It felt like forever lying there with him. We laid there in serene bliss, wrapped in one another's arms, crying at times for the loss we both experienced. We watched the day turn into night as the sun slipped below the horizon. Stars erupted in the sky above the burning field as we remained oblivious to the swirling smoke and ruin. The moon rose and set, and we didn't budge a muscle. Our hands rested on one another, and his chin never left my forehead. Every feeling I had felt for Xavier was now amplified twice as much regarding him. Twilight appeared on the horizon, and soon, the rising sun signaled that dawn was approaching. I felt my body growing light and realized the sleep meds that Starfire had given me were wearing off.

"See you on the other side?" I whispered.

"I will be waiting," he replied, kissing my forehead.

I awoke alone in my bed; the spot to my side was still sunken in where Xavier had laid with me hours before. I rose to my feet and made my way swiftly down the stairs to where Damian still sat chained and tied up in the chair I had left him in. I unshackled his hands and cut the rope from his body as he was still sleeping soundly. His face was peaceful and serene, almost looking as if a smile tugged the edge of his lips.

"Should you really be doing that?" Praeziel asked, breaking the quiet of the room and startling me.

"He's fine now," I calmly replied.

"For how long?" he asked.

"Alpha can never touch him again," I replied quietly, brushing his white locks from his face.

"Well, I hope for our sake, you are right," Praeziel retorted, standing to his feet and sheathing his sword. "Where is Xavier?" he asked.

"Xavier… is home," I replied, staring up into Praeziel's eyes.

He nodded, acknowledging what I meant. "The troops are to show up today. We all begin training with Starfire. It is my understanding that the warlocks will be fighting alongside us as well." He turned to leave through the door of the cottage when I called out his name.

"Praeziel?" I began.

He stopped and turned my way. "Yes?" he asked.

"I'm sorry," I replied.

"I know," he said.

"I also wanted to say thank you."

"For what?" he asked.

"For being you," I replied.

He looked a bit confused, and then he smiled and nodded, walking out the door. With strength I didn't have before, I lifted Damian from the chair he sat in and carried him up the stairs to my room, shutting the door behind me. I laid him down gently on my bed and sat beneath his head, stroking his hair. I figured he would have woken up by now. The sedative Starfire had given him must not have worn off yet. I watched him as his eyes rolled back and forth under his eyelids. I touched his cheek and stroked it, rubbing my thumb under his eye and down to his mouth. He began to stir, and for a brief moment, I was fearful that when he opened his eyes, he wouldn't be himself. However, no sooner had the thought crossed my mind than his eyes fluttered open, and I was gazing into the eyes of the universe.

"Welcome back," I murmured.

"Miss me?" he asked, reaching his hand up and touching my face.

"You already know the answer to that," I whispered, tugging at his locks.

He sat up on the bed, repositioned himself, and pulled me into his arms. I snuggled in close, breathing in his scent. I had never paid it attention before. He smelled like a meadow on a warm spring day. He shifted his position and leaned back against the headboard, pulling my body on top of his. We laid there snuggling, drinking each other in.

"Do you think we possess the power to freeze time?" I asked.

"We could try," he murmured.

"Think anyone else would notice?"

"No one but us would ever know."

I smiled at him and gently closed my eyes. Months of mental fatigue and physical exhaustion overcame me as I lay serenely in his arms. How long had it been since I was able to sleep a whole night without nightmares or being awakened by an attacking monster? I couldn't even fathom the number of days. I felt myself slip into darkness, the darkness in me finally at rest. A tranquil sense of calm washed over me as shooting stars and galaxies tumbled through my mind. They were no doubt vivid memories of what I had always wished to see. The viewpoint from the Summit that Xavier had witnessed, that I had witnessed all along. The dancing lights and swirling clouds of color put my mind at ease, and for the first time in a long time, I slept peacefully.

It was just a moment of respite. I was shaken awake by Damian as we heard the thunderous sounds outside. We slipped out of my room and ran down the stairs to the front door. Damian crashed through the door, nearly breaking it from its hinges. Hundreds of warlocks stood gathered outside, looking at the sky. We followed their gaze, shielding our eyes from the bright sun beaming down. Hundreds of meteors pelted against an invisible dome in the sky, crashing and burning upon impact. Stardust rained down from the burning rubble, filling the air.

More and more of Lightshade's people gathered, using their magic to protect their homes. They reinforced the barrier with each militant strike against it. I watched them all nearly deplete their magic and be replaced by another to carry on in their place.

"Alpha," Damian sneered.

"You are quite right," Starfire replied, walking up beside us and watching the sky. "He is angry."

"I took what was his," I replied, my eyes fluttering in Damian's direction. "This is my punishment."

"What can we do?" Damian asked, turning to Starfire.

She closed her eyes and smiled. "What you do best."

We both looked at her, confused.

"Shine."

Damian and I looked at one another, and he took my hand in his. The fiery glow of our souls erupted to the surface. He glowed his icy blue fire while I blazed in red and orange embers. We lifted from the ground, holding tightly to each other's hand. We each lifted our free hand, and light exploded, shooting across the valley. Our bodies grew brighter, and soon, nothing but pure white light was visible to the naked eye. The powerful glow gathered to the top of the sky in the center of where the magic dome encased the valley. Its tendrils slowly crept across the dome, latching onto every bit of magic that swirled above and solidified it in its place. It sparkled and crackled as it wound over and out across the entire paradise. We pushed hard with our light, and the descending meteors began to slow and hover in midair, suspended briefly before bursting into clouds of stardust.

Alpha's scowling face appeared in the sky, glaring intensely at me.

"Parlor tricks," he hissed.

"We're coming for you, Alpha," I replied. "You can try to run, you can try to hide, but we will find you, and you will fall like the ashes of Eden."

He laughed deeply. "Do you think you can take me alone? A handful of Nephilim and Warlocks? A meager fleet of angels. You will still fail in the end! My army grows by the day, and they are bloodthirsty." He smiled, rolling his head and cracking his neck. "Bow to me, and those you love will live in the end. Defy me, and well, nothing will be left to mourn. Not even you two."

Damian shot an icy fireball into the sky, and Alpha's face distorted and disappeared. We descended to the ground below, and those around us watched in awe. As our feet touched the ground, Praeziel walked up to us. He put his right arm across the center of his chest, then took a knee.

"I pledge my allegiance to you," he shouted. "I will follow you to the ends of the earth, no matter how soon or far off that may be."

We looked around at the growing numbers of people that stood in Lightshade. While we had been protecting it, the Nephilim had begun to arrive. One by one, each Nephilim that had entered the valley gathered around us, pledging their loyalty to Damian and me. The warlocks took a knee, yelling their allegiances into the air. We looked around in amazement as they, one by one, each announced to follow us to the end of days.

"We shall fight alongside you as well, young Shining Ones," a voice called out behind us.

We turned around to see the Seelie and Unseelie courts standing behind us. The Dark Queen Mab, Titania, and Oberon stood at the forefront of the gathered fey. All three of them bowed to us, and every single one of their followers followed as well. More and more people began to appear from various portals into Lightshade. The sun eclipsed to cast a shadowy glow across the valley.

"The vampires pledge our allegiance to the cause as well," replied a young man stepping forward. "For too long, Alpha has experimented with humans, turning us into nightwalkers with the vampiric blood of those in the abyss."

"The werewolves do as well," a young woman said, stepping into the front of the crowd. "Alpha has mistreated our kind for far too long. It is time he pays for the crimes he has committed against all."

I was overwhelmed by the support of every imaginable creature that had suffered from Alpha's reign of terror. I looked from face to face as millions stood before us, pledging their lives to stop him.

"We will follow you wherever you go," a voice said behind me.

I turned around and ran toward the voice.

"Daddy!" I shouted as I wrapped my arms around my father's neck.

He hugged me, tightening his grip around my shoulders.

"I have been so worried about you," I cried, tears spilling onto his chest. "I was so afraid that Alpha still had you and was torturing you as punishment to me."

"You don't know how good it feels to see you and know you are safe," he replied, pulling back from the embrace. "I never imagined in all the worlds that you would be so powerful."

"I get it from my father," I replied as he swiped away a falling tear.

Behind him stood thousands upon thousands of angels who had been left in the Summit when Alpha abandoned his throne in the sky. I scanned the crowd, looking for one particular face.

"She's not here," he said, knowing who I was looking for. "I will explain it all, but right now, we have business to attend to."

Damian walked over to join us, and my father patted him on the back.

"It's nice to see you again, kid," he said, smiling. "I see you kept to your word."

"Not quite," he murmured.

Dad looked at him, a bit confused. I knew exactly what he was referring to.

"Where's Xavier?" Dad asked, looking around in the crowd for his face as I had my mother's face.

"That's a long story," I replied gravely. "But for now, just know he is safe, and he is home."

"Welcome, Incaendiel," Starfire said, pushing through the crowd to stand face to face with him. He towered over her like a giant. "We have much to talk about and to do."

"Yes, we do," he replied, nodding in agreement. "It's my understanding you have something for me?"

"I do," she replied. "Follow me inside. I was hoping Sophie would be with you, but that was another alternative move in the vast game of chess."

Dad's eyes lowered. "Yes, I had hoped as well."

"Come now, don't doddle," she said, and we watched the two of them disappear into her cottage.

CHAPTER 7

THE SOUNDS OF SWORDS clashing against one another filled the air as training commenced in Lightshade. They trained in rotations, allowing the vampires and werewolves to train under the eclipse of the sun each day. Nephilim and angels, warlocks and Seelies all spent their days preparing for the ultimate battle with Alpha. Starfire had given my father his elixir, and he painfully drank it alone without my mother to take her dose. She had refused to leave Alpha's side.

Damian and I trained in hand-to-hand combat with one another as others stopped to watch and stare in amazement. We danced in a fiery ambiance as our skin glowed brighter and brighter each day, the haze of our powers never diminishing. We clicked our swords active and began to battle one another, him with his long sword and me with my dueling swords. Our weapons clanked against one another as we worked at a precision speed, gaining momentum with each thrust and parry.

"You had one helluva trainer," Dad said as he watched us.

"I sure did," I replied, smiling at Damian.

"Don't let her fool you," Damian said. "I'm really just hanging by a thread here. She is schooling me."

Dad laughed heartily. I saw a shine in his eyes I hadn't seen since I was a little girl. He liked Damian, not like he had a choice, really. I dropped my dueling knives and pulled on the hand-to-hand knives Reikal had given me.

"That is not fair," Damian said. "Those things amplify your powers."

"Is someone afraid of losing?" I giggled.

"I like a challenge," he mused, cocking his mouth into a side grin.

I readied my hands when a sudden pain tore through my chest. I pressed my fist into my chest, sinking to the ground.

"Luxina," Dad said at my side faster than a bolt of lightning. "What's wrong?" he demanded.

"I... I don't know," I choked out, the pain growing sharper.

It's Alpha, Xavier's voice called out into my head. *We made a mistake.*

"Xavier?" I asked out loud by accident.

Damian narrowed his eyes.

"Xavier? Is something wrong with him?" Dad asked.

My eyes slowly turned up to my dad's eyes. We hadn't told him about Xavier yet, just that he was safe.

"Not right now," Damian hissed.

"He needs to know the truth," I hissed, wincing as another pain tore through my chest. "It might be that!"

"It might be what? Tell me what?" Dad asked.

"Help me carry her inside," Damian said, lifting me up under one of my arms.

Dad grabbed me under the other and led me into Starfire's cottage. They sat me down in one of the chairs while Damian ran to grab me a glass of water.

"What do I need to know?" Dad demanded.

"There was a prophecy," I began.

155

"What prophecy?" Dad asked, shaking his head.

"The one about the birth of three Shining Ones. Except the third Shining One was never supposed to exist. When I was created, the power between you and mom split," I explained, clenching my jaw in pain. "I split in half. Part of me staying with you, the other part of me staying with mom."

"This doesn't explain anything about where Xavier is," Dad replied.

"Xavier was me, Dad. Xavier was the dark half of my soul," I said, pressing my hand harder into my chest as another wave of pain sliced through.

Realization spread across his face. "So, what happened?"

"I absorbed myself back," I replied quietly. "It happened a lot sooner than what we had hoped it would. But we had to save Damian from Alpha. He had hijacked his mind. It was the only way to save him."

"You sacrificed your brother to save him?" Dad seethed.

"Xavier sacrificed himself!" I yelled. "I sacrificed myself. You of all people should understand. Look at what you sacrificed for Mom! For a lie!"

"What do you mean a lie?" he asked, irritated.

"Ask your mother," I hissed. "It was all a lie. The search for the garden, your darkness leaching mom's light. None of it was true. Your mother played a power trip with both of you."

"Let me guess, he told you?" Dad asked, glaring at Damian. "It's lies, Luxina."

"He didn't tell me. He didn't have to. I know everything he knows. I can still hear the words echoing from the Dark Queen Mab's lips as she told him in the Otherworld," I hissed.

"Instead of arguing over what is truth and what is not, how about we focus on what is happening to Luxina?" Damian interrupted. "You can hate me later, but right now, she needs help."

"Indeed, she does," Starfire said, walking into the room. "Something went wrong with the absorption."

"Xavier told me it's Alpha doing it," I cried out, grabbing my chest as it felt like it was ripping from my chest.

"We know the poison from the injections was removed from Luxina by the Watchers. What about Xavier?" Starfire asked.

"No," Dad replied. "He wasn't dying from them."

"He had already absorbed them," Damian said. "After the first set he received, they no longer affected him."

"So, when she absorbed him, the poisons slowly began to re-enter her system," Starfire stated.

"Why didn't they burn away as mine did?" Damian asked.

"Because she was still transitioning and hadn't fully taken Xavier's soul into hers. The transition is complete now," Starfire replied. "That's why she can hear him now."

"Well, what do we do?" Dad asked. "We can't just let her writhe in pain."

"I'm afraid that's exactly what we have to do. She must filter it out of her system," Starfire said, setting the manacles we had tied Damian up with on the table.

"What are those for?!" Damian shouted.

"You know what they are for," Starfire retorted. "Now, put them on her. Alpha will work her the same way he did you."

"No," Damian replied, outright refusing. "We are not chaining her up. I can handle her."

"Damian," I croaked out. "Just do it."

"No," Damian hissed. "You are nothing like I was. You won't hurt us."

I rose to my feet against my will as if I were being controlled. Everyone took a step back from me.

"Everyone, leave the room," Damian demanded.

I watched as Starfire slowly backed away from me.

"No, no, over here," Damian said, jumping into my line of sight. "Get her out, Incaendiel."

"I'm not leaving this room," Dad replied.

"Just do it!" Damian shouted.

I turned to look at Dad as he walked calmly over to Starfire and stood in front of her as he helped her out of the cottage.

"Hey," Damian spoke softly. "Right here."

I returned my gaze to him, craning my neck as I stared at him. He held his hands up gently as if coaxing me out of a temper tantrum. My body moved forward even though I didn't want to. He stood his ground as I walked closer to him. I reached my hand out to touch his face, expecting him to flinch away. He did not.

"Your hair is white now," I said. I looked around the room, and we were the only ones left in here with the front door shut. "Where did Incaendiel go?" I asked.

"He escorted Starfire from the room," Damian replied nervously.

"Why? I wasn't going to hurt her," I said, walking around the room and touching everything.

"Luxina?" Damian asked. "Luxina, can you hear me?"

Yes, yes, I can! I shouted. But the words did not leave my lips. *Why can't I talk?*

Because someone else is controlling you, Xavier replied.

Who? I asked.

You already know who it is. Just dig deeper, Xavier said.

He was right. I did know.

"Come with me, Damian," I said calmly. "Come with me to where it is safe."

"I'm right where I need to be," Damian replied.

"Safe?" I laughed. "Do you think you are safe here? Safe with Luxina? She killed your brother. She took my Xavier from me, and she will take you from me as well."

"Sophie?" Damian asked.

"Yes," I replied. "It's me. It's mother."

"You're not my mother," Damian sneered. "You aren't anyone's mother."

"Don't talk to me like that!" My voice echoed off the walls with a deafening screech.

The door opened, and Dad walked back into the room. My eyes watched him close the door behind him and walk over to Damian's side.

"Incaendiel, you look so different now. Brighter, glowing," I whispered. "Why did you leave me?"

"I didn't leave you, Sophie," he replied. "You refused to go with me. Alpha has brainwashed you."

"Alpha is our one true father, and no one should come before him," I stated. "Why can't you see that?" My voice was pleading.

"No, Sophie. That is one thing that isn't true. We are our own gods and far more superior to him," Dad replied.

I felt the fury growing in me, and the haze of glowing skin burst into flames.

"She was more important to you than anyone else in the end. Even more important than my precious boy." I lifted my hand, and a flaming fireball formed. "I tried to tell you. I tried to make you see. But you refused to believe that your precious little baby was evil."

"She is not evil!" Damian yelled.

My head jerked to look at him. "She has you under a spell, son. She will kill you in the end, too. You're nothing but a monster to her."

No! He is not a monster! I screamed inside.

"I know her better than you think," Damian replied. "And she would never call me that."

I cackled, throwing my head back. "You are so naive," I cooed. "Alpha was right. You're nothing. You're weak. She has turned you into a mindless drone."

I tossed the fireball in my hand at Damian and struck him in the chest, knocking him to the ground.

What have you done? I whispered to myself.

Another fireball formed in my hand, and I looked at my dad. He stood there, calmly.

"You're not even going to fight back?" I asked. "Too afraid of harming your precious cargo?"

"I don't want to hurt you, Sophie," Dad replied, walking casually to me.

"Liar!" I screamed. "If you had never wanted to hurt me, you wouldn't have made a choice for me all those years ago. You would have come with me to the Summit, or I would have stayed with you at the Glade."

"Mother is to blame for that," Dad replied. "She lied to us, Sophie. She lied to lay claim to power in the little game she played with Alpha. And it just goes around and around, and it always claims us in the end. She wanted to control us. She needed to keep us apart so our power wouldn't overpower her own."

"No," I whimpered.

"Yes," he replied.

He stood before me with pleading eyes. He wrapped his arms around me and squeezed me tightly.

"I love you so much, Sophie," he said. "I never stopped loving you. And when I thought you loved another more than me, my love grew for you in leaps and bounds. Come to me, my love. Come and be with our children."

"Do you love him as your own?" I asked in a whisper.

"I was the one that saved him," he replied.

I felt something snap around my wrists. Damian had slipped the manacles onto my wrists while I was paying attention to Dad. I screamed in fury, and then everything went dark. When I woke up, I was tied in a chair, wrestling with the ropes that bound me. Damian sat in a chair directly in front of me as I had done with him. His head was bent down, resting in his hands. He looked up, tired, and just stared at me.

"Come back to me, Luxina," he whispered.

I'm right here! I shouted in my mind.

"I'm here for a while, so get used to it," I replied instead. "I don't understand why you care so much about her."

"You never will," he replied, annoyed.

"Then, explain it to me," I said snidely. "I have all the time in the world."

"The only person in this room that would understand is him," Damian said, pointing to my dad. "He loved you. He loved you more than life itself. He died and came back to life for you. I watched it happen."

"So, you would die for her?" I asked.

"Over and over and over, again and again, and again," Damian replied. "She saw me for more than a weapon. She saw me for more than just a chess piece. She loved me without condition. You... you chose Alpha over every person that loved you or that you loved. Luxina, she defied Alpha. You know she did. You were punished for it."

I stared at his face, studying him.

He is nothing like me, Sophie thought within. *How can he be so much like Incaendiel?*

"Because he knows right from wrong right now," Dad replied. "Alpha is injecting you with nothing more than mind-controlling substances. He has gained your trust in him through lies. You weren't strong enough to fight it. You aren't at fault for that. But you can't blame innocents for that. Luxina, she is innocent in all his. She is your daughter. That should mean something to you."

"There's nothing but cloudiness in my mind. All I can think of is hating her," I replied.

"That is Alpha thinking through you," Damian replied. "I know more than ever what that feels like."

"Save me," I pleaded. "Incaendiel, save me!"

Dad went to leave the room.

"No," Damian demanded, halting him in his steps. "This is a trick."

A deep laugh emerged from my throat.

"Oh, you were always the smart one," I said profoundly. "Did you know that at any moment I could just simply kill her?"

164

Damian's eyes widened.

"I love these little games we play too much to do that," I laughed.

Damian stood from his chair, kicking it across the room.

"You give her back," he demanded, yelling into my face.

"Tsk-tsk. Always with that temper," I replied coolly. "I was so sure she would never save you from me that you were mine in finality. But you loved her so much. You came back for her. Do you think she loves you as much as you do her?"

Yes, I do! I cried. *Don't listen to him, Damian.*

"If she didn't love me, she would have never tried as hard as she did to save me from you," Damian replied quietly.

"That is what you think or what you know? Could it be that she was using you as her own little weapon?" I asked.

"Don't listen to him, Damian," Dad said. "He will manipulate you and will use anything he thinks will make you weak."

"Luxina is already his weakness and has been since he learned who she was. Always fighting how he felt around her. Wanting her and her precious Xavier to stay together. I hold in my hand the only thing that will destroy him," I replied. "How do you save her when you couldn't even save yourself?"

Stop it! I shouted at Alpha.

"Join me, Damian," I said.

"I will die before I join you," Damian sneered.

"Then have fun rescuing your precious Luxina from the darkness," I said.

My head slumped forward. I was unable to move.

"Luxina?" Damian asked, running to me.

He grabbed my face in his hands, gently shaking it.

"Luxina?" he asked with growing worry in his voice.

I sat there numbly, unable to respond. He placed my hand to his face, covering his eyes as he sobbed. I wanted to answer him. I wanted to tell him everything would be ok, but I could not speak. I could just stare blankly ahead, aware of everything. A haze began to fall upon my vision as darkness descended in my mind. I tumbled and free-fell through a dark hole, thudding to the ground. I was back at the meadow. There was hardly any light here. The tree where I had met Xavier so many times was nearly burned to a crisp from the last time I was here. It still smoldered from the flames.

I sank to the ground and brought my knees to my chest. I gently rocked back and forth as I fought the panic and anxiety welling within my chest. This had been my greatest fear. Being utterly alone. I looked up to the sky, and the dark blankets that covered it didn't produce a single star. It looked as if someone had painted over it all with a large brush. I buried my face in my hands. I was lost. I didn't know how to find my way back to the light.

Luxina.

I could hear Damian's voice in the wind, but he would never be able to find me here.

Please, Luxina. I can't do this alone.

His voice was but a whisper in my ear. I sat there for hours listening to him plead with me. I tried to follow his voice quite a few times and just found myself back at the tree. I eventually gave up and just balled up on the ground. No one could help me here. No one could save me here. This was worse than the Lake of Fire. At least with the lake, I felt pain. I feel nothing here. It's almost as if I am a ghost walking through Sheol.

"That's a word I haven't heard in a long time," a familiar voice said.

I glanced up to see the smiling face of Xavier. I jumped from my feet and hugged him tightly. I cried into his chest.

"It's you," I breathed. "It's really you."

"Of course, it is me," he replied. "I am you, remember?"

"I didn't think I would ever hear you or even see you again," I replied, sniffling.

"You're not supposed to see me," he replied. "You're a long way away from the light."

"Alpha put me here," I replied. "He is punishing Damian."

"I know," Xavier replied. "I am here to help you get back to the light."

"You can't help me," I said. "No one can save me here."

"You don't ever pay attention to anything, do you?" Xavier asked. "I am the dark half of you. This right here, this is where I stay, in the quiet, dark abyss. But the abyss, it isn't bad. It's vast and deep, but it's not a death sentence. You, you're the light. You're the hope that keeps this place thriving. This place looks to you like a lighthouse in the dark. When the air is thin, and the darkness feels like it is suffocating, you are the call that lets it know that things will be ok."

I stared at him in his infinite wisdom.

"I told you I would be with you through it all. That means the good and the bad. And when things get dark, I am here to let you know that darkness is not forever. Because you make the shadows tolerable."

Luxina! I could hear Damian's voice, which had grown quiet a long time ago.

"His voice is back," I murmured.

"He is leading you home," Xavier replied.

"Where is home?" I asked.

"Where your heart is," he replied.

"Where my heart is…" I whispered. "My heart is with Damian."

"Then follow the sound of your heart," he replied. "It will lead you to the light."

"Will you come with me?" I asked.

"I will walk with you as far as the darkness lets me," he replied.

And he did. He walked with me through the dark as I listened for Damian's voice. Every now and then, it would be so loud, and then the sound would soften to barely a whisper. Xavier walked me through a garden that had all kinds of flowers that bloomed in the night air. White daffodils, azaleas, magnolia trees, and all kinds of white flowers bloomed here, lending some light to contrast the dark. When the darkness started to lift, we walked through a bed of tulips that started off white and then turned to crimson sprouts, and he stopped.

"This is as far as I can go," he said, holding my hand.

"What if I get lost or turned around?" I whimpered.

He smiled at me. "Just follow your heart. Trust your instincts." He bent down and picked up a tulip, handing it to me. I brought it to my nose and breathed in the sweet smell it emitted. It was partially white and partially red, split down the middle. "Tiptoe through the tulips. They are delicate and fragile but persistent and beautiful nonetheless, just like you."

He stood there, watching as I made my way to Damian's voice until I could no longer see him in the darkness.

Come back to me.

I am, Damian. Lead me back home to you.

I walked through more and more tulip beds that turned into a giant field under the light rays of the sun peeking through the clouds. The light became a blinding light, and I shielded my eyes as I continued to walk. I looked back toward the darkness where Xavier was.

Stay with me!

I paused, torn between the two. I looked at the blinding light and back to the darkness.

Stay with me…

His voice began to fade away. The light grew brighter and brighter as I ran headfirst into it.

Always, I replied.

CHAPTER 8

MY EYES FLUTTERED OPEN as sunlight filtered in an open window. I scanned through the room around me when my eyes landed on Damian slumped in a chair, sleeping. It wasn't often I was able to steal glances at him without him turning away from me. I drank in every single aspect of him I was able to see. Even as scars riddled his body, he was the most beautiful thing I had ever laid eyes on. Even if he refuted it himself, he would never be able to sway my made-up mind at how marvelous he looked. His white hair glistened in the rays of sunlight that filtered over him. And those eyes of his… They were remarkable pools of light in which I could spend all day basking in the ambiance of their glow.

I may have been forced to slip into the darkness where all seemed hopeless, but emerging into the light with him at my side was the best feeling in the world. It nearly felt like everything had been but just a dream. I got to speak with Xavier. I desperately needed to know that he was with me, and that question had been answered in the best way possible. I learned more about myself in my short time with Xavier than I had in my entire existence. Darkness was but a metaphor. There was nothing sinister about it. There was nothing about it that would harm me.

I began to stir in bed when Damian's eyes opened. I watched the recognition transform his glazed eyes to vibrant ones of joy and happiness. He rushed to the side of the bed and cupped his hands around my face, peering deeply into my eyes. His eyes wandered and searched every inch of my face as they came to rest on my eyes.

"I thought I had lost you," he murmured. "I was afraid you would never come back to me."

"I will always come back to you. I will always come back for you. I will always come back when it has anything to do with you," I replied, grazing his cheeks with my hand. "I heard your voice, and it led me back to the light. It led me back to you."

He leaned in and kissed my lips ever so gently. It felt like rose petals brushing up against them. I pressed back against his, and the fire built within my belly and bosom. I wrapped my arms tightly around his neck and pulled him deeper into the kiss as his body crashed down onto mine. All I cared about right now was showing him how much he meant to me. He was not a lost soul or a lost cause. He was not a monster. He wasn't Alpha's plaything. He was mine, and I was his, and there wasn't anything that anyone could do to stop it now.

I tugged his shirt off and up over his head, then ran my fingers all along his torso, memorizing every scar as if they were braille on his skin telling me a story. He wound his hand through my hair and flipped me over in the bed, where I was on top, pulling me in closer and closer with each labored breath of excitement. I settled beside him in the bed with his arms wrapped around me, binding me tightly to his chest.

"I could hear everything and see everything when they had control of me," I spoke softly.

"Yeah, I could, too," he murmured in reply.

"You know everything Alpha said to you was a lie, right?" I asked. "You do know I love you just as much as you love me, don't you?"

Damian fell silent.

"Damian?"

My eyes moved to meet his. He just lay there staring off at the wall behind me. I propped myself up on my elbow and gently caressed his chin with my hand, pulling his face to look at me. He couldn't maintain eye contact with me as his eyes gave away what he was thinking.

"I only think of you as one thing. It isn't a monster. It isn't a weapon. It isn't a chess piece. I think of you as beautiful. You're the most beautiful person I have ever met. Even before I knew Xavier was me, I had fallen in love with you. When you showed up at our campsite... I tried to fight everything I was feeling. But I couldn't. The more time I spent with you, the more I wanted to be with you. It was always more than just saving you from Alpha. I didn't want to save you because Alpha could use you as a weapon. I wanted to save you, to set you free."

His eyes locked on mine, and I could see the pain and anguish that Alpha had put him through. I could see how Alpha had convinced him time and time again that no one loved him. Had he waited for us to rescue him? Had he given up on us ever loving him? Had the doubt seeped deep enough that he would always question my love for him?

"I would have rescued you over and over and over again if given the chance," I whispered to him. "You're worth saving. You're worth loving. You're worth everything to me. You're my universe. Feel my love for you," I said as I placed his hand over my heart.

The room fell silent as I waited for him to speak. Everything in me felt like it was dying at once. My heart felt like it could wrench free from my chest and explode. How do you convince someone who feels worthless and loveless that they are the center of your world? That you love them unconditionally? That you see beauty where they believe ugly exists? How do you make them see through your eyes and experience what your heart feels for them?

He gently removed his hand from the center of my chest without a word. He stood up from the bed and walked to the door.

"When you feel up to it, we have training to do," he spoke softly.

He opened the door, walked out, and closed it behind himself. A range of emotions washed over me. How can you go from madly kissing someone to being distant and cold? Tears threatened to slip down my cheeks. I wiped them away, furious. I hated Alpha. I hated every single drop of pain he had caused my family to feel. I was going to make him pay, even if it meant I had to do it alone. He would regret every single moment he made Damian feel worthless and unloved.

I left my room and walked downstairs to the open door of Starfire's cottage. The Nephilim were training with the warlocks, and Damian was their leader. His skin glistened under the rays of the sun as he moved with diligence and ease. They mimicked his moves in unison.

"Nephilim were once powerful beings," Starfire offered, jarring me from my thoughts.

"What happened?" I asked.

"Alpha happened. They are half-mortal. They age exponentially slower than other mortals. They have immortal souls, but they do die. Alpha made sure that their immortality wouldn't last an earthly age. He stripped them of their immortality prior to the Great Flood, hoping they would all perish. Many did. The ones that survived had hidden away in Stygia with their mother. Many years after the flood, some decided to venture back out. They assimilated with humans. Some don't even know they are descendants of angels. The ones that stayed behind lived longer than the ones who did not," Starfire replied.

"Why?" I asked, confused.

"In order for them to retain their immortality, they had to pair up with another Nephilim. That was how Alpha stripped their immortality away. If they chose to take on humans as mates, they would live a human life. The ones that paired up lived forever. The ones that choose no side were met in the middle with death. They aged quite slowly, but eventually, they died. Once Alpha is defeated, they will be able to choose if they wish to be purely immortal or if they want to live mortal lives without being stuck in the middle of the two."

I watched the Nephilim soldiers as they picked up their swords and began to duel. I wondered which ones these were. Were they paired with other Nephilim, or were they paired with human mates? Were they paired at all? I caught Starfire watching me from the corner of my eye and turned to look at her.

"I know what you're thinking about doing," she stated.

"And what is that?" I asked innocently.

"You're going to try to stop Alpha all on your own. Kill him before the battle begins," she replied.

I turned my gaze from her and focused on Damian training those around him.

"He deserves to know that someone loves him enough to avenge what happened to him. What Alpha did to him," I said firmly.

"You know he won't let you go fight Alpha alone," Starfire chuckled. "He won't let you go at all."

I smiled. "That's why he's not going to find out," I replied.

"What are you going to do? Sneak off?" she asked.

"That's exactly what I'm going to do," I replied, shifting my body weight. "And you're not going to speak a word of this with anyone."

Starfire nodded. "Do you care if you live or die trying this?" she asked. "Because I know the answer."

I shook my head, staring back out at Damian. "No, I don't care either way. Just as long as he knows how much I really did love him. That's all that matters."

"Well, you better get a move on then," Starfire replied. "Training will be over soon."

I nodded and gave her a quick hug. I stepped out of the door frame so no one could see what I was doing. I pulled from deep within and summoned a portal. I had been to the compound Alpha had kept Damian. I was a prisoner there as well. I remembered the room they had held me captive in. It appeared in the translucent doorway. I stood there, staring through the open gateway. Could I really do this? Was I strong enough to really take down Alpha? Starfire knew, but honestly, I didn't want to know myself. I was a god now. I should be able to take on Alpha head-on and make it out alive. He couldn't even put Tiamat down. She still existed as the Leviathan. Just as I was about to step through, a voice called my name.

"Luxina?"

I looked over at Damian, standing in the doorway. He was puzzled, and his face gave away every bit of confusion he had. He looked at me and then looked through the portal to see where I was going. His face went from confused to fearful as he registered what I was doing.

"No!" he shouted.

"I love you, Damian," I said.

He ran toward me as I stepped through the portal, and the doorway disappeared behind me. I stood in the darkened room where, a year ago, I had been chained up with Xavier while Alpha tried to turn me into a war machine. This would be my only chance to make everything right again. I had to prove to Damian how much I cared. I had to show everyone that I was willing to take risks. I was not just a pretty face. I am my father's daughter. I had to prove that I was unbreakable.

"Ah, Luxina. You came back after all!"

I turned around to the voice that broke through the darkness.

"Hello, Alpha."

SNEAK PEEK AT BOOK 5

Firefly of Immortality II

Firefly of Immortality

I

THE GUARDIANS OF LIGHT SERIES

Kasey Hill

PROLOGUE

I SAT IN SILENCE as those around me bickered and argued. Half of them didn't want to engage with Alpha and half of them wanted to wage the war that had been long overdue. I sighed heavily as I squeezed the bridge of my nose in annoyance. I hadn't a clue as to why they weren't as furious with Alpha as I had been for the past millions of years. My emotions began to run rampant, and I could feel the burn bubbling to the surface. I had repressed my anger and resentment for far too long and it was ready to rear its ugly head.

"Why is it so hard to decide!" I yelled out, erupting into flames.

Silence fell over the quarreling room as all eyes rested on me. The flames receded as I composed myself. I looked at each face that sat in the room. The scars of war were painted on their skin. Runes of power etched their arms and faces. Their eyes… they told a story that no one could hear.

"You were all abandoned by Alpha. You were left to rot and for what? Doing your duty? Listening and doing what Alpha told you to do? You were all cast aside because he created something he himself could not destroy. You others," I stated, looking out toward the Nephilim in the room, "you were created from angels, and he turned his back on you calling you abominations! He loves no one but himself. He must be brought down to the level he deserves."

Glances were exchanged amongst themselves with quiet murmuring.

"Incaendiel is right," Sophia said standing from her seat. "We were made into Children of the Night. Alpha is growing his numbers by the day and soon, we will be battling replicas of ourselves that are evil, twisted, and manipulated into thinking we are the bad guys. That is Alpha does is manipulate others to bend to his will and if you don't, he will make you one way or another. Look at Incaendiel's poor daughter, Luxina. She stood against Alpha, and he nearly killed her with those injections. We need to stop his tyranny. We need to stop being afraid of the father that disallowed our entrance back into heaven. It is time to stand and fight. When the Seelie courts pledge their allegiance, we shall too. Both Watcher and Nephilim."

The room nodded as the murmuring grew to a loud hum and turned into boisterous chatter. I nodded to Sophia and smiled. I needed this. Alpha had taken so much away from me. Sophie had been the last straw. My heart sank as I thought of our last words before the Glade imploded. I balled my fists in fury and heartache. I would avenge whatever happened to her.

A loud siren began to echo throughout the war room, and everyone scrambled to their feet.

"What's going on?" I yelled over the noise to Sophia.

"Intruders," she yelled back. "Quick, we need to get the kids to safety!"

She began to run down a narrow hall that opened into an atrium. She disappeared down a corridor as I rounded the corner behind her. Hands snatched me from behind and before I could even react, I felt all my power drain from my body as someone wrapped around my wrists the one and only thing that could subdue all angels, something made from unicorn hair.

Chapter 1

IT HAD BEEN so long since I had seen daylight that I had forgotten what the sun looked like as a sliver of light seemed to find its way into the dungeon I had been locked away in. Time was a moot point, and there was no telling how long I had been left to rot in this cell. I had seen neither hide nor hair of Alpha or any of his minions since they had brought me to this place. It couldn't have been the place he wanted us to find him at. That would have been too easy. plus, the Watchers would have immediately executed a strike in retaliation to the bloodshed left behind when Alpha captured me. All I have been able to think of is if my babies were able to make it out safely. I know Sophia would never let anything happen to either of them. She knows more than the rest of us about what they are. She told me that we all are the key to saving the world as we know it before Alpha completely ruins it all with his new breed of angels.

It is so odd to think of me having more than one child when it has been Luxina and me solely for the last eight years. I saw the look on Xavier's face. He isn't too fond of me, but from my understanding, he isn't too fond of anyone except for Mother Lilith. She was the one that raised him while Sophie was off traipsing the galaxy for her son Damian. Just the thought of that little red-headed boy sent both sorrow and hatred through my bones. He was the reason Luxina was taken. However, he was also raised by Alpha without any choice. And the experiments Alpha has performed on him... the poor kid.

As if by cue, the door to this dreary place popped open, and in he strode. You couldn't mistake his fiery locks of curls on his head nor the astonishing blue eyes that shone like the stars. He was his mother made over. He didn't have a single feature of Lucifer about him, except maybe his attitude. I got a closer look at his face. His eyes were sunken in with dark circles under them. He was bone thin as well. Were they feeding him? Torturing him? I saw a red mark that trailed down his neck and under his shirt that looked fresh and was still bleeding a bit. He lingered at the door as if he were contemplating what he was doing. He straightened, and his demeanor changed. I waited for others to follow, but none did. He was alone, but that didn't erase the cocky smirk from his face as he shut the door behind him, walked over to me, and pulled a chair up sitting down and staring. I stared back, studying his face, trying to read his mind. He was a blank slate. *I wonder what Alpha wants him to do to me?*

"Nothing," he replied.

I know confusion had to spread across my face because he sat back in the chair, placing his arms behind his head and teetering the chair off its front legs.

"I know. It's confusing. And no, Alpha has no idea," he replied with a confident grin.

"You can read minds?" I asked in disbelief.

"Yes, but I haven't always been able to. I'm sure it is something that has to do with the experiments that Alpha does on me," he replied with a shrug. "It may have been the connection with my siblings that triggered it. I will never know. All I know is that one day, I could hear the thoughts of every person who stood in the room with me. Some may think it's a curse, some a blessing. I find it to be a useful asset in times of war."

"Your mother and I could read each other's minds. It might have something to do with that," I offered.

"She is not my mother," he replied heatedly.

I watched as he composed his anger and returned his gaze back to me. His face once again registered a cool, calm, collected look.

"Why do you say that, Damian? Why do you speak of Sophie in such ill regard?" I asked.

He looked away as a moment of sadness washed over his face before he could replace it with the cold, emotionless expression he liked to sport.

"She may have created me with my father, but neither of them will ever be my parents. They will never understand me. They will never understand the endured torture I have been put through while being with Alpha." He looked at me earnestly, and I nodded my head empathetically.

"You know, Luxina and you have that temper thing going for yourselves. She gets angered and explodes into fire so easily. I can't imagine who she gets that from," I replied with a chuckle.

"From my understanding, she gets it from you," he replied with a smirk.

"What does he want with me, Damian?" I asked.

"The same thing he wanted with me. The same thing he wanted with Sophie, and the same thing he wanted with my brother and sister," he replied. "He wants to build an army of new angels."

"I thought he no longer had the power to create? He can't just go around injecting people, hoping the injections take. And I certainly hope he doesn't think we can procreate a new race for him."

"He isn't going to do any of that," Damian replied with a sincere, concerned look.

"What are his plans?" I asked.

Damian looked around the room and leaned forward to me, the chair legs settling softly on the floor. "Once our blood accepts these injections, he plans to use Lilith at his side to create a special race from our newly formed blood. The creations won't be mindless anymore because he has Lilith at his side now. However, they thought the original werewolves and vampires were horrible in the beginning. These new creatures, these new angels he wants to make… they will destroy everything." He stared at me with bewilderment and fear.

"Why are you helping him?" I asked. "Why do you fear this plan but still help him?"

"I have no choice," he replied, straightening up and returning to his position in the chair he had been in. The nonchalant, not caring attitude washed back over him.

"We all have a choice, Damian," I replied. "There has to be a reason you are helping him."

"Who says I am truly helping him?" he replied with a sly grin.

"You helped him take Luxina and Xavier," I stammered in confusion.

"Incorrect. Lucifer was the one that orchestrated both of those incidents, not I," he replied. "I don't want them anywhere near Alpha."

"Afraid he would choose them over you, and you would be the outcast once more?" I asked, a bit too sarcastic. I expected him to fill with rage, but he did not.

"Yes," he replied very quietly and simply. "And they don't deserve that as a punishment."

It took me a moment to process what he meant by his last sentence.

"You care for them, don't you?" I asked, squinting at him.

"Why wouldn't I? They are what I am missing in life. They are my blood," he replied. "I keep everyone at arm's length. I don't wish to get close to anyone. It's been my thing since I was a youngster. Alpha never showed me what love is. He never showered me with affection. He just wanted me to create this stupid army of his. However, I have seen the way Luxina looks at me. She looks at me with love, empathy, and sorrow. She doesn't see me as a monster. At least, she didn't until the attack of the Watchers. I have no idea what her thoughts of me are at this moment. She could hate me for all I care. All that matters is that she and Xavier stay safe and as far away from Alpha as I can keep them."

"So, when you took her from me, all those things you said. Your cold demeanor... that wasn't you?" I asked.

He shook his head. "The injections Alpha gives me make me vulnerable to mind control. I must do whatever I am told. Lucifer struck a deal with Alpha to deliver both Xavier and Luxina to him in exchange for me. Alpha took the deal, but he won't hold up his end of the bargain even if he still had them in his grasp. Alpha needs us."

"Mother created us. She can create more of us. Why does he need us in specific?" I asked.

"Because the Unseelie Queen will no longer help him, nor will she aid Lilith in creating more of the Shining Ones," Damian replied, shifting in his seat. "She is the key to it all..."

"How?" I began when the door busted open.

Lucifer walked in, grinning ear to ear. "Ah, son, starting early, are we?" he asked, walking over to Damian. "Did Alpha give the orders to start on him?"

"Yes and no," Damian replied, settling his chair back on the ground and standing up. "We were just having a small chat. I needed to know where my siblings might be hiding and who, but their father would know that answer. However, you interrupted."

A voice echoed in my head. *I will return again to speak with you. I have a lot to fill you in on before things get so out of hand that they cannot be controlled. There will be another visitor, and after they leave, I will be back to free you.* I looked at Damian, who was staring intently at me. I nodded with my eyes.

"Well, does he know where they are? Do we need to force it out of him?" Lucifer asked, grinning madly.

"He doesn't know," Damian replied, walking to the door.

"And you believe him?" Lucifer shouted.

Damian spun on his heels and pinned Lucifer against the wall. "Do you question my authority?" Damian demanded, glaring at Lucifer. "He doesn't know."

I could see the fear settling on Lucifer's face and nearly grinned. That boy does hate him, and who could blame him? He was dealt a crappy hand by this whole thing.

"That is not how you talk to me! I am your superior, and I am your father! You will respect me!" Lucifer bellowed.

"Respect is earned, and you do not have a single respectable bone in your pathetic existence," Damian retorted.

"Is that why you're in here? Buttering up to Incaendiel in hopes he would adopt you as his?" Lucifer demanded.

"At least he proves to be a better father than you ever have," Damian seethed. "Now, leave the room and do not bother the prisoner. Alpha wants him to remain untouched and unharmed. Those are orders!"

And with that, Damian left the room. Lucifer scowled in my direction and followed, shutting the door behind him. Once again, I was left in the dark, dank room with everything whirling around in my head. Could that be it? Could Damian be looking to me as a father figure? I processed everything we had spoken about. I believed him. His fear of what Alpha was planning was real. I believed he was being forced into doing what Alpha wanted. He wanted to be free. If I ever escaped this hell hole, I was going to be the one to free him, too. I owed it to Sophie. I owed it to her memory. I owed it to her soul. She had spent so long searching for him to get him back. I had to save him just for her. She wasn't here to do it herself...

One thing that Damian had said bothered me the most. He spoke as if he had seen the chaos and destruction of the future if Alpha were to succeed in making this new race of angels. He had the ability to read minds; could he see the future as well? Did all the children have this gift? When did it start? I know Luxina would have mentioned hearing people's thoughts if she could, but I had just met Xavier before I was seized. I didn't even get a moment to speak with him really. Is he like Damian? Did he have unique gifts as well? Does Damian dream like the twins do? These were all questions I needed answers to and couldn't even go to search for them. I was trapped here. I knew if I pulled hard enough on the chains, they would break free from the wall, but what good would that do? I would still have to fight my way free. If they captured me once, they could do it again. My only choice was to sit here and wait for Alpha to appear and share his grand plans with me. Damian gave me a taste of what the plans are, and I needed more than that. I needed to see who my visitor would be.

At the sight of Damian, I couldn't help but be consumed with thoughts of Sophie. Grief overtook me as I sat there thinking of the only person I had and would ever love. I had spent millennia trying to convince her mortal mind and heart to love me once more. As fast as I had gotten her back, I had lost her. I agree with Luxina that it wasn't fair of me to let her go. Lucifer wasn't supposed to hurt her, either. When I had seen her locked away in that tower, so helpless, so vulnerable, every empathetic fiber for Lucifer snapped within me. After he orchestrated the kidnapping of Luxina, my blood boiled regarding him.

The last few moments I had with Sophie were… the most painful ones I had ever experienced. Wanting to wrap her in my arms and float off into eternity was thwarted, for I had more pressing issues at hand than my own selfish love interests. Our children needed to be saved. What bothered me the most, though, was when Luxina broke free of the nightmares inflicted by the injections Alpha gave to her she said they were of her mother speaking to her. Her mother blamed her as she burned in the fire. Was it possible that Sophie's soul spoke beyond the potter's field of angels? Our last words together, she was enraged, thinking I only wanted to keep Luxina safe and not Xavier. As if I would let my own son be harmed in any way. I had no clue I had a son until I was informed by Lucifer right before he took Luxina.

The Watchers told me that Luxina spoke of burning in a lake of fire in her moments of lucid talking. Was it possible that Sophia was also in that lake? Could Sophie have genuinely reached out to Luxina? Was Alpha punishing Sophie for Luxina escaping with Xavier? Dozens of thoughts flooded my mind, and I couldn't even escape them. The one that lingered the heaviest though was who my visitor would be.

Chapter 2

I SAT UP GROGGILY with my vision zoning in and out to light and then black. Little flecks of light darted around in the black and I sucked a gulp of air into my lungs. As my eyes came into focus, I surveyed my surroundings. I had no idea where I was or how I got there. I touched the back of my head and winced in pain, withdrawing my hand that had blood smeared on it. What happened? I tried to focus my thoughts on one single moment, but everything was a blur. The last coherent thing I remembered was chatting with Damian, and Lucifer busting in. I tried to concentrate on what we had been talking about, but my mind was foggy.

My eyes still circled the area where I lay. I looked down to see exactly where I sat to see if there were any clues as to how I got here or what I was doing here or even why my head was bashed in. A soft bed of peat moss with pink and purple flowers growing all around it lay beneath me. My eyes moved out a bit further than where I sat and noticed that there was a circle of stones around the bed of moss. *Circle of stones…. Circle of stones… I know there is….* I tried to think hard and remember what a circle of stones in the forest meant. The harder I tried to think, the worse my headache hurt.

"I can fix that up for you, love," a voice cooed in the wind ever so softly.

I whipped my head around trying to see who it was. My eyes began to unfocus and blur again with the blackness threatening to take over.

"Do you know how you got here?"

The voice was a female voice, melodic and soothing. I tried focusing again, looking around. My eyes landed on what looked like a small woman. I squinted to try and ease the blurriness of my double vision.

"I can't remember anything," I replied as I tried to stand.

Nausea and dizziness overtook me, and I sank back into the ring of moss. *Ring of moss... circle of stones... faery circle...*

"Are things coming into focus now?" she asked, stepping closer but still maintaining her distance.

"You're a faery," I blurted out.

She giggled. "Aye, that I am. But do you know which faery?" she asked, chiding.

"If I knew which faery, I would have said your name," I replied, irritated and a bit snarky.

"I'm not just some measly sprite or brownie, now. I'm a real faery with some real power to my punch. I'm fey, part of the Seelie court," she offered.

Seelie court... it can't be...

"You wouldn't happen to be the Queen herself, would you?" I asked, attempting to stand to my feet once more.

"You're a quick one, Incaendiel," she replied. "Aye, it is I, Queen Titania."

"How do you know my name?" I asked, walking over to her with wobbly legs and a loud thump on my head.

"I know all about you. You're a Shining One, just like your children are. Sweet lad and lass you have there," she smiled.

"You've met Xavier and Luxina?" I asked with mixed emotion.

"Of course I have," she replied with a giggle. "Come with me, and I will tell you all about it."

She extended her hand to me, but I hesitated for a moment about taking it. The fey have never provoked the celestial realm, never caused any trouble with angels or fallen angels, but they could be nefarious, whether they were Seelie or not. I weighed my options. I could stay here, wherever here was, and try to find some way to go where I needed to go, even though I couldn't remember where that was supposed to be. Or I could go with her, and she might be able to fill me in on what exactly was going on.

I took her hand, and she smiled as she walked me through a meadow. Birch trees wrapped around us as we walked, and either my vision was still weird from the hit to my head, or there was something weird about how our surroundings looked. They look ... warped.

"That is the portal you see," Titania replied as if she knew what I was thinking. "Birch tree groves are direct portal paths to the Seelie court."

SNEAK PEEK AT BOOK 6

BLACK WINGS OF DEATH

PROLOGUE

WHY DO I HAVE to be so stupid? Why am I all of a sudden so damn insecure around Luxina? All the abuse Alpha put me through weakened me instead of strengthening me. Around her, I didn't have my feet on the ground. I had no stability. I free floated. It was amazing and nerve-wracking all at once. I wanted to give her everything, and at the same time, I was afraid of the world being jerked out from beneath my feet.

How could she love me so much as hideous as I look? There was some truth behind what Alpha had said through her. She didn't need me here because she wanted me. She required me to be away from Alpha so I wouldn't be his weapon of mass destruction. She had said it herself. She needed me this. She needed me that. She can't just all of a sudden *want* me.

"Take it easy, Damian. We're training, not really fighting," Praeziel yelled, ducking from my sword.

I snapped from my thoughts, nodding apologetically. "My head's not in it right now," I replied.

"It's ok. Training for the day is over anyway," Praeziel offered sympathetically. "How is Luxina?"

"Awake," I sighed.

"Why are you out here with us and not in there with her?" Praeziel chided.

I didn't answer as I shoved my weapons back into my bag. "You let him get to you, didn't you?" Praeziel asked.

"Who?" I asked, pulling my shirt back on.

"Alpha. When he had control over her, he said something that got to you, didn't he? About her?" Praeziel continued.

"Maybe. So what?" I huffed.

"Whatever it was, don't believe it. Don't let it sink in. You go back in there to her and forget everything. Don't break the bond you two have," Praeziel reassured.

"I'm not... breaking the bond. I just have

some things to work through. It has nothing to do with her. It's all me," I replied.

"Well, don't let her think otherwise. She's more vulnerable now than she was before. She has the dark half of her soul back. It can consume her easier than most because she's never experienced it before," Praeziel warned.

"Yeah," I replied. "I hadn't thought of that."

I dropped my bag on the porch of Starfire's cabin and walked through the doorway. Luxina stood in front of one of her portals. Where was she going? Was Starfire sending her somewhere? Why hadn't she told me anything about it?

"Luxina?"

Luxina glanced back at me with determination in her eyes. I looked past her to see where she was going. On the other side of the portal doorway was a darkened room. As I stared closer, I could see chains on the wall, and a flickering light bulb was lighting the room up quickly every so often and shooting it back into darkness. I knew that room. I knew that place.

"No!" I shouted.

"I love you, Damian," she said.

She stepped through the portal faster than I could get to her side. It closed behind her as I tried to jump through at the last minute. I thudded to the floor.

"No, no, no, no, no, no!" I shouted over and over, pounding my fist into the floor.

I rolled from all fours over to a sitting position with my hands cupping my head. Fear tore through my body. I had to get to her. I had to get to her before Alpha got his hands on her. Anxiety ran through my veins, and I felt weak momentarily. Starfire calmly walked to the center of the floor.

"Why didn't you tell me she would do this?" I seethed, jumping up to my feet in anger.

"Because I didn't know how this day would have gone. There were two possibilities. The first one was that when she woke up and told you how much she loved you, you would welcome it with open arms. The second possibility is what happened. You put up a wall," Starfire replied.

"Why did she go? How does this have anything to do with…"

It sank in. Luxina wouldn't just risk going to Alpha unless she had a plan. Her reasons for going had to be simple enough, but at the same time, they had to mean something more than just going for revenge or blood. She was going for one specific reason.

"Do you see now why, Damian?" Starfire asked.

I looked up at Starfire with tears welling,

forcing them back down. "To prove how much she loves me," I choked out.

"So, you know you can't stop her. She's going to do this or die trying, but you won't be able to stop what she is doing," Starfire offered.

"Then, we will both die together," I avowed through gritted teeth. "I'm not letting her do this alone."

"You'll never find them, Damian..."

CHAPTER 1

STARFIRE WAS RIGHT. I left immediately from Lightshade and made my way to Alpha's lair at Chernobyl. By the time I had gotten there, everyone had already packed up and left. All that was left behind were remnants of the experiments Alpha had been conducting. Bodies lay dead, rotting in the cells they had been held in as prisoners. The Forsaken were scattered throughout the entire building from whatever fight had taken place. This place had long since been abandoned. *Why would Alpha have sat around*

waiting in here? Had he been controlling her still, somehow, someway? None of it made sense.

I scoured through all the rubble that was left behind from the Forsaken fighting against one another. They had all chosen a side, the leader they wanted to follow. Some chose Alpha, and some chose me. Once again, brother had been pitted against brother. I made my way to Alpha's office and slid the door open slowly. I glanced around on edge expecting to be caught going into his office unattended. The room was a wreck. I picked through papers lying aimlessly on the floor, trying to find where Alpha could have gone, but I came up empty-handed. I walked to his desk and rummaged through what files sat on the top of the desk.

Anger tore through me, and I swiped everything off with my hands. A lamp and miscellaneous items hit the floor with a thud as I braced myself against the desk fighting back the urge to smash every- thing in the room. *They should have been here! Why weren't they here?!*

My eye caught a piece of paper sticking out from one of the drawers. I tried to open it, but it was locked. I grabbed hold of the drawer and yanked it hard, breaking the mechanism that kept it in place. It slid open, and my eyes landed on a gold mine of information.

Every single creature, beast, and experiment Alpha had created and conducted was in this drawer. I pulled out the heaping stacks of papers and plopped them on the desk. I grabbed the seat of the chair that he haplessly sat in while he worked from behind the desk and began to skim through all his notes. Every single thing he had made was cataloged with what injection was given, what type of creature from which it was bred. It had a list of their weaknesses, their strengths, and whatever special powers he had given them were also included.

I rummaged around in a closet off from the desk and found a duffel bag. I quickly shoved all the information I had acquired into the bag to take back with me to Lightshade. We would have the upper hand with this kind of knowledge. I looked in the drawer once more and found a few more things. There were the plans for the iron heart I had seen in a brief glance last time I was in here. I stuffed that in the bag along with all the other files at the bottom of the drawer. As I lifted the last bit of paper, I noticed the bottom of the drawer had a false bottom to it. I carefully pried it up just in case it was a spring trap and stood back, awaiting some sort of climactic ambush as the last attempt from Alpha to stifle me.

Nothing happened. I leaned over the drawer and peered inside it to see what was so crucial that Alpha had to hide it at the bottom of a locked drawer. There was a large box at the bottom. I picked the box up and turned it over in my hands. It didn't have a lock to open it with a key. It looked as if it had no seams for a lid either. *How do you even open it?* I shrugged and stuffed the box in the bag as well, then zipped it up. As I was about to walk out of the room, I noticed a map on the wall with different pinpoints marked with pushpins. They were all unusual colors and dispersed over the entire planet. I grabbed a pen from the floor and a piece of paper that I had thrown from the desk and began to trace the map taking note of longitude and latitude points where the pushpins were placed. After I had a rough copy of the chart, I flicked my fingers and lit the papers on the floor on fire. No one would use this building ever again if I had any say in it.

The room roared to life as the fire quickly ate the paper, and soon, the fire raged inside the room, eating it alive. I quickly snaked my way through the halls and out of the building as the fire chased after me. I sat in the meadow and watched my prison burnt to the ground in earth-shattering explosions with glee. Whatever chemicals had been stored there by the humans were flammable and gave no mercy to the structure that held them captive.

"I figured I would find you here," Praeziel called out over the roaring flames.

"Starfire was right," I declared in defeat. "They weren't here." "We'll find her," Praeziel consoled. "Together."

He extended his hand out to me and helped me to my feet. I grabbed the duffel bag of paperwork I had snagged from inside and tossed it over my shoulder. Praeziel and I hadn't spoken much in the last couple of days. He hadn't said much at all since Gwendolyn... well... since we found out about her betrayal.

"What's in the sack?" he asked, staring at it. "A monster," I smirked.

He scowled, squinted his eyes, and

furrowed his brows in annoyance as I chuckled.

"It's paperwork Alpha had hidden away in his desk drawer. He cataloged every single thing he ever created or experimented on with a thorough list of useful information we could use to defeat them," I replied.

"Yea?" Praeziel asked, surprised.

I nodded. "I also have the blueprint of that iron heart I had caught a glimpse of before. I bet that is what he put in that giant iron, what- ever," I stammered.

"We'll give them a look over when we get back to Lightshade. We need to get a move on before the fire draws attention to this place while we are still here. There's no telling who Alpha has staking this place out. For all we know, he controls the mortals around here as well to guard the place," Praeziel warned as he began to walk from Chernobyl.

"What's so bad about mortals?" I chided.

"I am not allowed to harm them even in defense," Praeziel replied. "We took an oath never to harm our kindred."

"Oh, well, that would be problematic, then," I offered. "Let's get going."

We started trudging our way through the

meadow. It was so like the one near Potter's Field that I found myself lost in thought, remembering the last time I had been there. It was when Luxina and Xavier became one to save me. She tried so hard to free me from Alpha, and I let him get inside my head, knowing very well that she loved me and wanted me. When she touched my forehead, I felt every single emotion she had ever felt toward me. Every memory of me flowed through my mind. She had loved me without even knowing she loved me. And when I saw her crumpled on the ground, the field and tree on fire from her self-destructive emotions after absorbing Xavier, I felt helpless, hopeless. But I felt everything from her. I should have never let words replace what I had actually felt from her.

A strange noise snapped me from my thoughts as Praeziel and I came to a halt walking through the towering wheatgrass. We both scoured the field as the wind blew, the wheatgrass bending back and forth in the slight breeze. We stood still and silent for a moment without seeing anything that matched whatever we had heard. We began our silent trudge, paying closer attention to our surroundings.

"Something doesn't feel right," Praeziel whispered, taking each step carefully and methodically through the field.

"I completely agree," I mumbled, glancing back and forth.

There was nothing but this tall wheatgrass for acres. There weren't too many spots to exactly hide unless whatever tripped our senses was lying like guerillas in the grass waiting to pounce. An almost electrical feeling filled the air along with a type of hum.

"I know that sound," I mumbled. "We need to leave now!"

Kasey Hill has lived in Franklin County, VA, for most of her adult life and is a versatile writer known for her work in several genres, including urban fantasy, horror, thriller, paranormal romance, and metaphysical/New Age topics. She has authored both fiction and non-fiction, with a particular interest in Wicca, specializing in Trinitarian Wicca as the historical archivist with an upcoming historical account of the shift from polytheism to monotheism in Abrahamic religions, where she has published non-fiction works exploring the subject.

Her fiction often dives into the supernatural and the macabre, blending mythological elements with modern storytelling. She has published multiple novels, poetry collections, and short stories. Notable works include her *Guardians of Light* series in the mythology fantasy genre, and her poetry that has received recognition for its depth and emotional resonance. As she grows in the horror genre, she has a particular penchant for Southern Gothic storytelling, such as her Adult Horror novel *Devil's Claw* and her Young Adult horror series, *The Whispering Spirits* featuring *The Haunting at Foxwood Village* and *Dark Coven*. She has several

Horror short stories circulating for anthologies and Ezines featuring her unique style of worldbuilding.

In addition to her writing, Kasey Hill has also contributed to the Wiccan and occult community through her non-fiction work, making her a multi-faceted author with a broad range of interests and expertise.